The Granny Project

www.randomhousechildrens.co.uk

Also by Anne Fine

Published by Corgi Books:
The Book Of The Banshee • The Granny Project
On The Summerhouse Steps • The Road Of Bones
Round Behind The Ice House • The Devil Walks • The Stone Menagerie
Up On Cloud Nine • Blood Family • Blue Moon Day

Published by Corgi Yearling Books:
Bad Dreams • Charm School • Frozen Billy
The More The Merrier • Eating Things On Sticks • Trouble in Toadpool

A Shame to Miss . . .
Three Collections Of Poetry
Perfect Poems For Young Readers • Ideal Poems For Middle Readers
Irresistible Poetry For Young Adults

OTHER BOOKS BY ANNE FINE

For junior readers:
The Angel Of Nitshill Road • Anneli The Art-Hater
Bill's New Frock • The Chicken Gave It To Me • The Country Pancake
Crummy Mummy And Me • Genie, Genie, Genie
How To Write Really Badly • Ivan The Terrible
The Killer Cat's Birthday Bash • The Killer Cat Runs Away
Loudmouth Louis • A Pack Of Liars • Stories Of Jamie And Angus

For young people:
Flour Babies • Goggle-Eyes • Madame Doubtfire
Step By Wicked Step • The Tulip Touch • Very Different

For adult readers:
All Bones And Lies • Fly In The Ointment • The Killjoy
Raking The Ashes • Taking The Devil's Advice
Telling Liddy • Our Precious Lulu • In Cold Domain

www.annefine.co.uk
www.myhomelibrary.org

The Granny Project

ANNE FINE

CORGI YEARLING

THE GRANNY PROJECT
A CORGI YEARLING BOOK 978 0 552 55438 1

First published in Great Britain in 1983 by Methuen Children's Books Ltd
Published by Egmont Books, 2002

Updated edition published by Corgi Books,
an imprint of Random House Children's Publishers UK
A Penguin Random House Company

Penguin
Random House
UK

This edition published 2006

13

Text copyright © Anne Fine, 1983, 2006

The right of Anne Fine to be identified as the author of this work has been asserted in
accordance with the Copyright, Designs and Patents Act 1988.

All rights reserved. No part of this publication may be reproduced, stored in a retrieval
system, or transmitted in any form or by any means, electronic, mechanical, photocopying,
recording or otherwise, without the prior permission of the publishers.

Penguin Random House is committed to a sustainable future for
our business, our readers and our planet. This book is made from
Forest Stewardship Council® certified paper.

MIX
Paper from
responsible sources
FSC® C018179

Corgi Books are published by Random House Children's Publishers UK,
61-63 Uxbridge Road, London, W5 5SA

www.**randomhousechildrens**.co.uk
www.**totallyrandombooks**.co.uk
www.**randomhouse**.co.uk

Addresses for companies within The Random House Group Limited can be found at:
www.randomhouse.co.uk/offices.htm

THE RANDOM HOUSE GROUP Limited Reg. No. 954009

A CIP catalogue record for this book is available from the British Library.

Printed and bound in Great Britain by Clays Ltd, Elcograf S.p.A

For Boris

'Stupid and Greedy . . .'

A visit from the doctor

The doctor was having a hard time with the Harris family. He'd been around to their house often enough before, of course. He'd been their family doctor for years. He'd seen them bellowing red-faced in cots, or miserably picking at their chicken poxes, or coughing horribly in steamed-up bathrooms. He'd never seen them all together in one room, and well, before.

The noise was appalling. The four of them, two girls, two boys, sat round the kitchen table eating like wolves. There was much scraping of knives and grating of forks. All the plates rattled on the table top. They were, the doctor realized after a moment's perplexed reflection, all seconds, warped in the kiln and sold off cheaply in the market. The children didn't seem to notice the clatter, or that their plates were wobbling horribly. They sat, hunched over, eating very fast. The elder boy's last sausage, stabbed too hard, spun off the plate onto the floor where he immediately swooped to stab it with his fork again.

'No need to kill your food. It is already dead.'

The beautiful Natasha Dolgorova spoke from where she leaned, distant and contemptuous, against the airing-cupboard door.

The doctor sighed. You'd never think she was their mother, he thought. She acted as if they were nothing at all to do with her, some horrible mistake, just for today, this houseful of children; as if the next-door roof had blown off in the night and she, a cool exotic childless woman, was just for once forced into looking after them.

'Nor is it poisoned. And so you need not spit it on the plate.'

'That's *gristle*, that is!'

'Tsssk!'

She hissed so fiercely, the doctor jumped. None of the children took the slightest notice. The doctor hurriedly went on with filling in the form in front of him.

'Osteoarthritis,' he muttered, scribbling in yet another large blank. 'Metacarpophalangeal joint involvement leading to characteristic volar sub-luxation and ulnar deviation of the phalanges...'

'What?'

Henry Harris, the children's father, sunk in gloom beside the vegetable rack, was suddenly deeply suspicious.

'He says your old mother's fingers are bent.'

'Ah.'

'Degenerative changes in the cochlea...'

'And she goes deaf.'

'Right.'

'Impairment of brain tissue function with concomitant deterioration of cognitive functioning...'

'And stupid, too.'

'Natasha!'

'Tsssk!'

The doctor kept his head well down.

'She's still smart enough to get to the newspaper every morning before anyone else,' Sophie said.

'What's in a newspaper to interest you?' Natasha demanded of her elder daughter.

'Stuff. Stuff for projects. Any old stuff.'

Her brother, Ivan, laughed through his mouthful of chips.

'Everything interests me and Sophie,' he said. 'Now we do Social Science. Crime, Violence, Police Corruption and Consumer Protection, Race Relations, Suicide Rates, Sex Statistics—'

'Tsssk!' Natasha Dolgorova hissed at her son who, grinning, tossed his dark curls back at her and calmly went on sopping up leftover ketchup with his bread.

'Projects! Pah! Such a school! I'll take you out of it! *Projects!*'

'There's no specific ambulatory problems, I take it.'

'The lazy old woman can still walk, yes. If she is truly hungry.'

The doctor winced.

'More of a shuffle, really,' Sophie said.

'Well, that's because she stole my bedroom slippers,' Henry Harris explained to the doctor mournfully. 'They're several sizes too large for her feet.'

'Her dietary intake?'

'The woman can eat *anything.*'

The depth of Natasha's scorn was unmistakable.

'It's true,' Henry Harris had to admit.

'She ate the leaves off Sophie's geranium last week,' Ivan said, troublemaking. 'And Nicholas and Tanya caught her chewing feathers this morning.'

'You did?' Natasha asked the younger pair.

'A few,' said Nicholas, playing it down.

'Lots,' Tanya declared, exaggerating.

'See! Stupid and greedy, that is what she is!'

'Natasha! Please!'

'And she should know the *cost* of pillows.'

'Ssssh.'

'*Tssssk*, yourself, Henry Harris! She is not *my* mother!'

The doctor, folding back another side of paper, suddenly spotted the end of the form. He cheered enough to say:

'One further manifestation, should we seek it, of the proven versatility of the human gastro-intestinal tract.'

'Just what I said,' Natasha Dolgorova claimed. 'The woman can eat anything.'

The doctor rose. He tapped the forms.

'I'll see that these get to the right place,' he said. 'But since there's no immediate problem—' Catching one of Natasha's venomous looks he hastily amended this to – 'Since Mrs Harris isn't actually ill at present, results may not be immediate, you understand. But I'll do what I can.'

The children all stopped clattering to lift their heads and look at him. Then Ivan said:

'What does he mean? Results? What's going on? Are you two thinking of putting Granny into a Home?'

'Thinking is finished,' Natasha told him. 'It is decided.'

'Dad?'

Henry Harris blushed.

'*Dad?*'

'Your mother and I are finding Granny an enormous strain,' he began.

'You're never sending Granny *away*?'

'Nothing's *decided*,' Henry Harris said uncomfortably. 'Nothing for you to worry about. Let's wait and see.'

Natasha hurled the dirty dishes into the sink.

' Шипа в мешке не утаишь,' she said darkly.

'What? What did she say? Dad, what did she just say? What was that?'

The panic was traditional. Natasha's proverbs were notorious.

Sometimes it appeared to Henry that the only thing his wife had brought with her when she moved west across a frozen continent was a seemingly inexhaustible supply of ominous sayings.

'What did that mean, Dad?'

'Nothing.'

'*Dad!*'

Henry Harris dropped his head in shame, and translated:

'You can't hide sharp steel spikes in soft cloth bags.'

'Do we care?'

The Granny project

The children held their meeting at the back of the garage. Sophie let Ivan take the comfy tyre and sat down on the upturned tea-chest. Tanya and Nicholas perched on the bonnet of the car.

'First thing,' said Ivan. 'Do we care?'

Four hands went up.

'Next thing,' said Ivan. 'Do we believe that we can stop them?'

Four hands went up again.

'Last thing,' said Ivan. 'How?'

The pause that followed did not last for long. Tanya suggested frequent bouts of tears, and screaming nightmares featuring Granny chained to an iron bedstead in the Home, starving and lonely, missing them all. Ivan put forward the idea of a strike: not fetching in the coal, no washing-up, refusals to run down to the shops. Nicholas thought that the strike should go further, that they should all refuse to speak, except to one another or Granny, until the whole idea was dropped for good. Sophie was silent, still thinking hard, till all of their ideas ran out and they turned round to look at her.

'Well?' Ivan said. 'Sophie?'

'Listen,' said Sophie. 'This project that was set last week—'

'For Social Science?'

'Yes.'

'Well?'

'You and me, Ivan, we'll team up for it. We'll work together, doing a joint project, double the length.'

'On?'

'Ageing people in the community.'

Ivan began to grin. Tanya and Nicholas looked blank. Sophie went on:

'We'll get the statistics stuff from newspapers and books and the Web. That won't take long. But half the project, a good half of it, will be a fairly vivid and uncensored description—'

Ivan broke in:

'Of one particular family!'

'An illustration of the fundamental stresses—'

'Features—'

'*And* issues,'

'The economic,'

'Social,'

'And psycho-social—'

'Pressures which underlie this growing trend—'

'Of taking ageing—'

'Non-functional!—'

'Members of the family unit,'

'And relocating them,'

'Along with their peers,'

'In Leisure Homes!'

'A case study,'

'In depth,'

'Of one particular set—'

'Of family dynamics.'

'The *Harris* Family!'

'That's it.'

'Oh, well done, Sophie! Well done! Well done!'

Ivan's eyes shone, Sophie looked rather proud of herself. Tanya and Nicholas, uncomprehending and forlorn, began to complain.

'What about *us*?'

'It's not *our* fault we don't do Social Science yet.'

'You two,' said Sophie, 'are to be responsible for keeping up the pressure. Two bursts of tears each, every week, with no explanation. One screaming nightmare each, every week, with just the slightest hint of Granny. No more than that, no details at all. No starving old ladies chained to iron bedsteads, Tanya. Just tears and creeping fears. Ivan and I will take time off from working on the project to rehearse each of you before your performances—'

'And we'll draw up your schedules—'

'To co-ordinate with ours,'

'For maximum effect.'

'Right!'

Tanya cheered up at once, her dignity restored. Inwardly she began to plan her first lurid nocturnal fit of hysterics. Nicholas, not quite so easily mollified, said rather sullenly:

'I still think you two are planning to leave Tanya and me out of this, just because we're younger.'

'What do you mean?'

'Well, all those *words*, for one thing.'

'Those are just Social Science words.'

'So what *is* Social Science, anyway?'

'Stuff. It's just stuff.'

'What *sort* of stuff?'

'All sorts of stuff. Civil disobedience, Voting patterns, Attitudes to rape and bottle-recycling and abortion, Teenage spending patterns, Causes of urban decay and hypothermia in senior citizens, Links between vandalism in city parks and high unemployment. Just stuff.'

'Why do they call it Social Science, then?'

'You can't expect them,' Sophie replied, 'simply to call it *Stuff.*'

A wreath for Harry Rowe

As Henry Harris carried the six empty milk bottles along the hall that night, he bumped into his mother, who was shuffling slowly backwards out of her room.

Mrs Harris smiled with delight at meeting her son so unexpectedly. She wore a cast-off dressing gown of Henry's, tied loosely with a flower-patterned belt from one of her best Oxfam dresses. Upon her feet were Henry's bedroom slippers held in place by wide red elastic bands dropped on the doorstep by the postman. The morning newspaper was clamped under her arm, and on her head she wore a badly moulting feather hat.

'Hello there, Mum,' said Henry Harris. 'What are you up to at this time of night?'

Mrs Harris rooted anxiously inside her purse.

'I'm off to buy a wreath for Harry Rowe,' she confided.

'He's not dead yet.'

'I'll put all your names on the card as well.'

'But he's not *dead*.'

'I'll get a good one.' Mrs Harris delved some more among her loose coins. 'About three pounds?'

'Not a wreath, Mum. Perhaps some flowers. I suppose there's a faint chance he might be feeling a little unwell . . .'

'I prefer a *wreath*, Henry. I'll choose a nice one.'

Henry looked out of the front door into the pitch-black night. He wondered momentarily whether to open battle on another front – the fact that the florist closed several hours ago – and then decided not to bother.

'You can't send Harry Rowe a wreath while he's alive.'

'Perhaps a nice one in the shape of a cross?'

'I'll get it.'

And Henry, sighing heavily, tucked two of the milk bottles under his left arm, slid a third onto a spare little finger, and held out his free hand. Mrs Harris, pleased and relieved, handed her bead purse over to him, and shuffled back inside her room.

Henry walked out of the front door and shut it, with enormous restraint, quietly behind him. He put the milk bottles down on the step, then crept round the house and climbed back in through the kitchen window. As he tiptoed silently along the hall, past the closed door to his mother's room, he caught sight of Ivan sitting on the stairs and writing something in a bright yellow notebook.

'Shouldn't you be in bed?' he demanded. 'What are you doing, anyway?'

'Just taking notes,' Ivan explained. 'Notes for a project. How do you spell Rowe? Does it have an e?'

Statistics

Sophie sat on the bedroom floor beside Ivan, her knees drawn up to support the bright yellow notebook she was writing in, her back against the door. She sucked her pencil, thinking, for a while, and then began to write:

Until recently, most old people lucky enough to have children were looked after in the family till they died. Then various social changes, for example

Sophie paused, and then, impatient to get on, muttered:

'For example, blank, blank, blankety-blank and blank,' as she wrote:

(_____, _____, _____ and _____) changed all that. Statistics show the percentage of people in Britain over _____ years old has steadily risen, for reasons of

'Blank, blank, blankety-blank and blank...'

_____, _____._____ and _____
from ___% back in 19___ to ___% now. The
number of Homes for Old People also rose.
Back in 19___, ___% of people over the age of
were cared for at home. However, by 19___,
fewer than ___% were living with their
families.

'You can't say that,' said Ivan. 'That sort of thing will simply *encourage* them.'
'True.'
Sophie crossed out the whole of the last sentence. After a moment's thought, she substituted:

However, in spite of the very real difficulties
of keeping an old person in the home, of
the ___,000 people over the age of___in Britain
today, as many as ____% are still living safely
in the bosom of their own families.

'That's better,' Ivan said.
He went back to copying down the list of blanks that Sophie needed him to fill, with careful researching.
Sophie went on:

The problems of having an old person in the home are legion

'No,' Ivan said. 'They'll think you copied that straight out of a book.'
'Manifold?'
'No.'
'Myriad?'
'Don't be silly, Sophie. That's worse.'
So Sophie put a line through what she'd written, and wrote instead:

There are certainly a lot of problems in having an old person in the home.

'That's better,' Ivan said.

And our project will deal with these under the headings: economic, social, emotional, physical, medical

'Blank, blank, blankety-blank,' prompted Ivan.

_____, _____, _____ and _____,

Sophie wrote.

By investigating these problems we hope to understand what lies behind the statistical trend we have noted. We chose to study one family in particular,

'The Harris family.'

the Harris family, because they so neatly illustrate the phalanx of problems involved.

'Sophie . . .'
Sophie crossed through the last few words and substituted:

so many of the problems involved.

Sophie put down her pencil.
'I'll leave the rest,' she said. 'Until you've done a bit of searching about on the topic. You might find something we don't know about already that we should fit in somewhere.'
'Right ho, comrade.'
Ivan put on his shoes and went to find his library card. Left to herself, Sophie looked phalanx up in the dictionary.
'Pity,' she muttered to herself. 'Shame, that.'

The first bloom of youth

Natasha swept the carpet around Mrs Harris's armchair, muttering black curses learned early at her peasant grandmother's knee and hysterically swiping burnt toast crumbs from one end of the carpet to the other. Ivan dutifully dusted his way around the clutter of small china ornaments on the dresser. Mrs Harris sat imperturbably, her snow-white hair in a freshly washed shock around her wrinkled face, the cat asleep on her knees.

'I really must get a job,' she declared.

'Would you like to begin by cleaning your room?' Natasha asked, a shade unpleasantly.

'No fear,' said Mrs Harris. 'Not so long as I can watch you two do it.'

Ivan grinned. Natasha pretended that she hadn't heard. After a while, Mrs Harris said:

'I put your present there on the dresser, dear.'

Ivan could see there was no present on the dresser. Natasha, caught off-guard, said:

'What present?'

'For your birthday, dear.'

'It's not my birthday.'

'It is the fourth of May today, isn't it?'

Natasha gazed out of the window into the thick November fog and considered. She could say yes. She could say no.

'Yes.'

'Then it's your birthday. Happy birthday, dear.'

'Thank you.'

'Yes, happy birthday, Mum,' said Ivan.

'Tsssk!'

Natasha leaned upon the broom handle. 'If you don't mind,' she said to Mrs Harris, 'I'll wait to open it.'

'That's fine, dear.'

Natasha added, under her breath, so only Ivan heard:

'Until the twenty-seventh of July.'

She swept the crumbs into the dustpan. Mrs Harris said:

'Which one is it, dear? I've forgotten.'

'Which what?'

'Which birthday?'

'Oh, that.' Natasha stood for a while, considering. 'It is my seventeenth,' she decided.

'Oh, really, dear?' Mrs Harris smiled fondly at her. 'Seventeen! Fancy!'

Natasha carried the dustpan and broom towards the door.

'Seventeen,' Mrs Harris repeated gently. 'I hope you know that you will soon be past the first bloom of youth.'

An accident

Natasha hurled the bundle of soiled sheets onto the kitchen floor, in front of the washing machine.

'That's it!' she shrieked. 'The end! She goes, or I go!'

The children all sat as still as waxworks round the table. Henry laid down the newspaper and got to his feet.

'I'll do them,' he said. 'My turn, anyway.'

He stuffed the stained damp sheets, one after another, into the machine while all the children watched him covertly. He sprinkled washing powder in the drawer, and poured a good amount of disinfectant in after. He shut the front and spun the dials. The small red light came on. The huge white gleaming machine clicked into life. There was the sound of rushing, filling water, and then the calming and comforting rumble of strong machinery coping efficiently spread through the kitchen.

'There!' Henry said.

The children dipped into their ice cream again.

Natasha threw herself against the airing-cupboard door. 'Christ!' she shouted, beating the wooden panels with her clenched fists. 'Dirty old woman! Christ!'

'They do have special sheets,' said Henry. 'For when these things become a real problem. I'll get in touch with the health visitor. I'll phone some-one up about it tomorrow morning, my love. Promise, I promise.'

She let him prise her off the door and lead her to a chair. She sat quite still, her face drawn, for a moment, and then, dropping her head upon her arms, she began sobbing.

One by one, as the children finished eating, they left the table and the room. Though the large tub of ice cream sat, still half full, on the draining board, nobody asked for more. Tanya and Nicholas went into the back room and switched on the television. Ivan went out of the front door. Sophie went up the stairs into her bedroom. She shut the door behind her carefully, and taking the bright yellow notebook out of her desk, flicked through until she found the page she had entitled *Physical Problems.*

On the first clear line she wrote: *Extra bed-changing.* And under that: *Soiled sheets.*

She felt intensely disloyal to her mother as she wrote the words, and half inclined to rub them out again.

Nicholas's nightmare

Nicholas woke when Ivan prodded him. He tried to snuggle straight back under the warm duvet into sleep again, but Ivan persisted, digging his fingers into Nicholas's shoulder.

'All right,' muttered Nicholas. 'All right.'

'Now you be careful,' Ivan warned him. 'Don't you get carried away. Stick to the script. Granny. Crying. And that's all. Right?'

'All *right!*'

'Sssshh!'

Ivan crept out, leaving the door sufficiently ajar for noise to carry through the house. Nicholas gave his brother a moment or two to get back safely into his own room, and then began to scream, first nervously, then, once he was committed, with fervour.

Beds creaked. Doors banged. He kept on screaming, on and on.

Natasha rushed, barefooted, into his room. She scooped him up into her arms. 'Nicky,' she said. 'Nicky?'

He grabbed her tight, she held him tighter. She squeezed him till the breath came out of him. She rocked him backwards and forwards, soothing him, rubbing his back. 'Nicky, Nicholas. Ssshhh. Nicky. Nicky.' She slid her hand under the back of his pyjamas and stroked up and down the ridge of his spine. It felt so warm and comforting he would have sunk back into sleep again, if she'd not asked him:

'Hey? What's all this? Bad dreams?'

He nodded, nestling closer against her. Her nightdress smelled of soap.

'Bears? Wolves? Soldiers? What's getting at my Nicholas? Tell me.'

'Granny.'

'Granny? Getting at you? Never!'

'Not *getting* at me. She was *crying*. Big tears. Huge great big tears.'

Natasha rocked him back and forth, back and forth, rubbing him still.

'Your granny's sleeping. Sleeping like a baby. Like you should sleep.'

'But she was *crying*.'

'Life can be sad.'

Nicholas had, suddenly, questions to ask. But he had promised Ivan he would stick to the script, and so he said again:

'But she was *crying*.'

'So she was crying,' Natasha said. 'There are things to cry about in life. Жизнь прожнть – не поле перейти.'

'What's that?' said Nicholas. 'What did you say?'

'Sleep now.'

'What did you *say*?'

'Жизнь прожнть – не поле перейти,' Natasha said once more. 'To live life's not so simple as to cross a field.'

And as she rocked him, on and on, Nicholas drifted back into sleep, across a wide field.

Her democratic right and duty

'What do you mean, my mother wants to vote? She hasn't voted since she came to live with us.'

Henry Harris, frazzled from a bad day's teaching, depressed beyond measure at the prospect of the next government, dolloped great lumps of mashed potato onto one plate after another, and passed them to Natasha. Natasha stared at each plate as if she'd never seen mashed potato before, ladled on stew, then passed them quickly on to Ivan, who distributed them around the table, to the extent of passing the last two plates back to his parents.

'She *can't* vote.'

And Henry Harris raised his voice to carry over Nicholas and Tanya's bickering about the pepper, and reach the far end of the table where Mrs Harris sat, bolt upright, dressed in her outdoor coat and balding feathered hat, eating mashed potato.

'You can't vote, Mother,' Henry announced.

Ivan gave Sophie a quick warning look across the table, but she'd already leaned back a little in her chair, getting ready. Under the table Ivan stretched out a foot to touch his brother gently on the shin. Nicholas obediently broke off his squabble with Tanya and, shifting his chair a little closer to the table, he covered Sophie who surreptitiously began to write in the bright yellow notebook under the table as Henry Harris said again in challenging tones:

'You can't vote, Mother, and that's that!'

Everyone looked towards Mrs Harris. She, concentrating hard on her new teeth, which she found prone to slipping about inside her mouth, carried on eating meat and potatoes.

'See!' Henry crowed. 'Vote? Her? There'd be no point. No point at all. She lost her grasp of the subtleties of British politics before the Falklands War. She hasn't bothered to vote in years, not even when I begged her to last time and the time before. Her? Vote tonight? *Ridiculous!*'

Seeing the circle of deeply disapproving faces around him, he broadened his attack to include them.

'Who *told* her, anyway? Which one of you was daft enough to mention to her that today is Election Day?'

Tanya said coldly:

'There's a large sign gone up outside her

window. It says: *To Polling Station.*'

'Is there, indeed?'

Henry appeared to be about to go and uproot it.

Natasha said:

'Lucky to be where voting counts. So if your old mother wants to vote, she should vote.'

'*Why* should she vote?' Henry half screamed. 'She has no concept of the issues!'

'Issues!' Natasha scoffed. 'A British General Election fought on issues? Is it a chilly day in Hell?'

Henry flushed scarlet.

'Well, *I'm* not taking her down to the polling station,' he declared. 'I'm just not doing it. She doesn't really want to go anyhow. It's freezing out there. She's forgotten. It was a whim. What difference does it make to her which lot gets in, now pensioners are sacred cows. I'd understand it if she read the papers. She doesn't, though. She simply nips out there at crack of dawn and swoops on them before the rest of us are about, then keeps them clamped under her armpits for days on end. So far as I can make out from her conversation, she never actually *reads* them. She doesn't know a thing about what's going on. I very much doubt if she could tell you the name of the Prime Minister. There's absolutely no point in discussing it further. She's dropped the whole idea in any case. She can just take her coat and that god-awful feather hat off and sit and watch it all on telly as usual. Go out and vote at eighty-seven! Good heavens above! I wouldn't mind if she weren't *senile*, but as it is she can just—'

At this point in her son's tirade, Mrs Harris stopped chewing to swallow the large lump of meat that had been worrying her. She shifted her new teeth back into their most comfortable position and, unaccountably, her ears cleared just in time for her to hear him saying:

'She can just go back in her nice warm room and stay there!'

'Oh, no, dear,' Mrs Harris said. 'Not tonight, Henry. It's good of you to worry about me, but I have wrapped up well.'

'Mother—'

'Henry! It is my democratic right and duty to vote!'

Sophie was so impressed she broke off taking notes under the table and stared, like the others, at her grandmother.

Natasha laughed.

Henry glowered horribly.

'It's all right for you,' he hissed at her under his breath. 'You've *never* cared what people think! You'd think that you still lived in Novosibirsk for all the notice you ever take of what goes on in Bonnington Road!'

Bonnington Road – bastion of democracy

The polling booths were set up in the local primary school. When Sophie and Ivan asked if they could come along, Henry simply assumed it was some kind of nostalgic pilgrimage they were making. He failed to notice the bright yellow notebook tucked under his daughter's arm as she walked through the doors in front of him.

'Bonnington Road – bastion of democracy!' Henry scoffed. He held his mother's arm as she shuffled with some difficulty along the smooth tiled floors in the enormous carpet slippers, moulting blue feathers on all the conscientious citizens behind her. The senior presiding official overheard as he passed the small group on his return from the lavatory to the assembly hall. Plucking a livid feather off his lapel, he glanced back at the small group of them suspiciously – one clearly senile, two clearly under voting age and one self-confessed anarchist. He kept his eyes peeled for the rest of the evening for unattended bags.

In front of the swing doors, Sophie stopped and laid Mrs Harris's heavy outdoor shoes down on the floor in front of her.

'Do you want to change now?' she asked her grandmother. 'Or are you going to vote in your slippers?'

'*My* slippers,' Henry Harris reminded the world.

'I'll try, dear,' Mrs Harris said. 'I'll try. It's just my feet have spread so in these.' She added, somewhat accusingly, to Henry: 'They're *far* too big.'

'They fit *me*,' Henry Harris countered. But Mrs Harris, ignoring him, took both the slippers Sophie handed up to her and stuck them firmly into her handbag. With Sophie's help she stuffed her swollen feet into her outdoor shoes. Then, taking Henry's arm again, she clumped into the voting hall.

'You two can wait outside,' Henry said hopefully.

'That's all right,' Sophie said. 'We don't mind waiting here.'

'We'd like to watch democracy in action,' said Ivan. 'You never know when you'll be covering it, in some project.'

Henry approached the women at the official table.

'One hundred and fifty-two, Bonnington Road,' he declared. 'Henry Harris and Adelaide Harris.'

'Would that be Henry *Alvin* Harris?'

'That's right.'

Sophie and Ivan looked at one another, and smiled.

'And Adelaide *Priscilla* Harris?'

Henry prodded his mother in the ribs.

'Don't poke me, Henry,' Mrs Harris said.

One of the women handed a fresh white ballot paper to each of them.

'Thank you, young woman,' said Mrs Harris. Both of her stockings slid down around her ankles. Henry just looked away, aghast, but Sophie darted forward and, while everyone tactfully looked the other way, tucked them both back under the ancient, shrivelled garters.

'There,' Sophie said. 'All systems go.'

'Come on, Mother,' Henry Harris said grimly. Under the eyes of several officials, and all the brisker voters moving in and out, he half led, half pushed his mother across the room towards the polling booths along the wall.

'Don't push me, Henry,' Mrs Harris said, and one leg of her enormous bloomers fell down below her knee.

The presiding official spoke softly to the woman beside him.

'They think he dragged her here against her will,' Sophie whispered to Ivan.

'To get one more vote for the party he supports.'

'A poor old woman.'

'Practically lame. Can't even walk here in her shoes.'

'It's probably an electoral offence.'

'One of the things officials here are trained to look out for.'

'So they can notify the relevant authorities.'

Across the hall floated the voice of Mrs Harris: 'Henry? Where do I put my cross?'

The room went suddenly quiet. Nobody moved. The silence lasted while Henry tried to speak, then cleared his throat, then tried again.

'Wherever you choose to put it, Mother,' he croaked.

Each strangled word was heard by everybody in the hall, so still were they all standing, so hard were they all listening.

Mrs Harris disappeared once more inside the little polling booth.

Henry Harris folded his ballot paper in half. Avoiding meeting the officials' eyes, he pushed it through the slot in the ballot box and went to stand between his children. They waited together in silence until Mrs Harris at last re-emerged. She stood, blinking in the light, uncertain what to do next, the ballot paper waving in her hand. Since Henry made no move to go and help her, Sophie again took over. She walked across and took her grandmother's arm, and steered her over to the ballot box. Under the eyes of the officials, as if to prove there was no sleight of hand going on here, she prised the ballot paper from between the old lady's fingers, folded it as she had seen her father fold his, and pushed it into the ballot box.

'There!' Sophie said.

The officials sat – silent, impassive.

'Come on, Gran,' Sophie said. 'Duty done.'

Defeat

Later that night, when all the television pundits were predicting that Henry Harris's political party was about to spend a full five years out in the political wilderness, he blamed his mother.

'I blame my mother,' Henry Harris said. 'It's senile people like her, who don't know which way up a ballot paper goes, who bring in land-slide victories for this bloody lot, time and again.'

Sophie looked up from the bright yellow notebook in which she had just written, upon the page headed *Physical Problems*:

Even a seemingly simple thing, like exercising his or her democratic rights and duties, can put an absolutely enormous physical strain upon the old person.

'It wasn't Granny's fault this lot got in. She never voted for them.'

'How do you know?'

'I saw her ballot paper when I folded it.'

'Who did she vote for then? The Bring Back the Birch candidate?'

'No one.'

'No one? What do you mean, no one? I saw her voting.'

'She put the cross exactly on the line between the top two candidates.'

'*What?* Spoiled her vote?'

'She didn't have her spectacles on.'

'After all that *effort*? That *trouble*? All that *humiliation* with the slippers? *Wasted* her vote?'

'I suppose so.'

'I'll kill her. I will *kill* her. I *will.*'

As Henry Harris sat, head in hands, mumbling death threats, the pundits on the television set spoke of four more safe northern seats that had gone down in the political landslide. Sophie looked down at the yellow notebook in her lap and read through the last words she had written:

exercising his or her democratic rights and duties, can put an absolutely enormous physical strain upon the old person.

She looked across at her defeated, miserable father, and in a sudden burst of filial sympathy, she changed the last full stop into a comma, and added on the words:

and other members of the family.

Ivan came in.

'Tanya is sleeping rather restlessly,' he said. 'Tossing and turning in her bed.'

'Well she may,' Henry Harris said. 'With five years of this lot in office, well may we all toss in our beds tonight.' He shuddered. 'After all that,' he said again. 'A wasted vote!'

Natasha rustled last Friday's newspaper, the most recent she'd been able to find that day, over the Women's Page to the Business Section.

'Lucky to be where there is voting at all,' she remarked.

Maximum impact

'You *can't* let Tanya have her nightmare tonight.'

Sophie had come across the two of them rehearsing in the garage. Ivan replied:

'Of course she must. Maximum impact, Sophie.'

'But it's their party! Their one and only dinner party. They've cooked and cleaned and fussed all day, and now you're going to *spoil* it.'

'That's all the better. Don't you see?'

'No, I *don't* see.'

Sophie sat down on the old flowerpots. She watched as Tanya, loving every minute, ran through the nightmare she would have tonight – the shout that would chill everyone who heard it, the staring empty eyes still lost in dream, the broken sentences: '. . . looking so frightened . . . being tugged further and further away from us . . . calling our names . . . Granny, of course . . . no, I can't remember any more . . .'

'You mind you don't,' warned Ivan. 'No embroidery.'

'That's very good,' Sophie admitted.

Tanya ran off.

'Ivan,' said Sophie. 'We just can't do this. We simply cannot do something that will ruin this dinner party of theirs tonight. I saw her on her knees this morning, scrubbing the muck off the kitchen floor. He's been down to the shops a dozen times since lunch, for bay leaves and extra cream and a replacement bulb for that bathroom light. He's in there now, still cooking, you know. She ironed a shirt for him to wear tonight. She even made Nicholas shine her best earrings with silver polish. There are fresh cut flowers in the living room. Do you know how much fresh cut flowers cost? This is their one bash of the year, Ivan. She's repaying hospitality to all those nice people who give her their spare tickets to concerts and plays, and offer her room in their cars when they go to London, and send her pupils for conversation classes, and pass on their children's school blazers to us. He's trying to keep his end up in front of the headmaster, and stop that Higgins who is ten years younger than him becoming head of Language Studies. She's vacuumed the whole house, even under the chairs and the sofa. He's bought six different kinds of drink. Six! She's gnawing her nails in there, cursing the colour of the carpet, the pudding, her own hair.

He's got so nervous, he's getting egg yolks into his whites, over and over.' Sophie leaned forward and held her hands out to her brother. 'Ivan. We just can't do this to them. We *can't*.'

'Sophie,' he said. 'It's all decided. We voted on it a long time ago. The Granny Project is well under way. Already we've all spent hours and hours on it. We're doing this for a cause we believe in, not for ourselves. We're doing this for a defenceless old lady who's too far gone to help herself. What is one interrupted dinner party for them compared with several years alone in some Home for poor old Granny? Think, Sophie. Think!'

'I *am* thinking.'

'No, you're not. That's very clear. You're only *feeling*.'

'That isn't necessarily worse.'

'It isn't *thinking*, though, is it?'

'So? Maybe you should try it for a change!'

It was the closest they had come to quarrelling in some time.

Due to a temporary fault . . .

Mrs Harris was settled down that evening much earlier than usual. Henry brought in her customary glass of sherry at half-past four instead of seven. Natasha served her supper – a heavy meal of pizza and suet treacle pudding, both favourites – a little after a quarter-past five. A second, larger, sherry followed at six. At seven, seeing his mother's head nodding, Henry deftly pulled the television plug out of the socket in the skirting board. The screen went blank.

'That strike's on, then,' said Henry. 'Bloody trade unions.'

'Strike?' Mrs Harris said. 'What? On every channel?'

'Afraid so, Mum.'

'Oh, dear. How very disappointing.' She brightened suddenly. 'Well, never mind. At least it's Saturday.'

Henry thought fast. Which night was slimmest pickings on the radio?

'Tuesday,' he said. 'Tuesday, tonight.'

'Is it? I could have *sworn* that man said Saturday.'

'Tuesday.'

'Look in the paper, Henry. Read it out for me.'

Henry tugged that day's paper out from where it was still clamped, under her arm. He said, looking with interest at an article on football on the Sports Page:

'*Analysis.* Then after that it's *Investment News and Views.* Then *Economic Growth Patterns in Prague,* followed by *Yesterday in Parliament.* Later, they have—'

'Never mind, dear,' Mrs Harris said, defeated.

She went to bed like a lamb.

Sophie, emerging from behind the door, picked up the newspaper herself. She wondered later, reading it upstairs, if her father had felt the slightest pang of guilt unplugging the television upon the very night they were to show *The Royal Command Variety Performance.*

Eight o'clock

The sound of guests arriving filled the house. Car engines died outside. Doors slammed. The bell kept ringing. There were two telephone calls from people circling around Bonnington Close and Crescent, Lane and Avenue. The unfamiliar voices rose to the landing where all the children sat, out of sight.

'So *lovely*! Natasha!'

'*George pensait que nous étions perdus!*'

'Shall I just go through? Is there anyone in there?'

'Henry! An ironed shirt! How splendid!'

'Доорый ычер.'

'Where you turn left into Bonnington Drive, before that Bonnington Street turns into Bonnington Mall.'

'Oh, gosh! Is that drink all for me? It's enormous!'

Tanya and Nicholas peered through the banisters. Sophie and Ivan shared the newspaper.

'We'll be like that some day,' said Tanya.

'I hope there are more leftovers than last year. They never seem to make enough spare. It's always mostly gone the next morning.'

'Food like they cooked today must cost the earth.'

'He had to queue twice at the cash machine.'

'I can see right between that woman's breasts.'

Ivan put down his half of newspaper, and crawled across.

'Be fair. You're looking almost directly down on her,' he said judicially, after a while.

'*And* so is Daddy.'

They were sent off the landing in fits of giggles. The guests thought what a merry open bunch they seemed, compared with their own difficult and secretive children. They put it down to cultural differences, Natasha being Russian.

Omelettes and eggs

Up on the landing, Sophie listened with interest to the brief bright patches of conversation that floated up whenever the dining-room door opened to let out Henry with a tumbled pile of plates, or let Natasha in with yet another marvellous array of food. She sat in the unusual warmth and brightness, happy to hear the gaiety in Natasha's voice, relieved to spot the tiny complacent conspiratorial nods that passed between her parents as they crossed in the hall.

So everything was going beautifully. Well, *good*.

'Ivan.'

She leaned back, tapping on the bathroom door.

'Ivan!'

'What is it? I'm not finished yet.'

'When you come out I want to talk to you.'

'About our Tanya's dream tonight, is it?'

'That's right.'

'Chicken!'

When Ivan finally emerged, Sophie said to him:

'It isn't chicken, Ivan. It's a decision.'

'You can't make unilateral decisions.'

'You'll just have to agree with me, then.'

'What sort of compromise is *that*?'

'Ivan, if you don't agree to our stopping Tanya spoiling their evening, I shall do it myself. I shall. And after that, I shall back out of the whole Granny Project.'

She looked down, to avoid his scorn.

'It is,' she said, 'a matter of principle for me.'

He laughed, as she had known he would.

'What principle? The principle that if a thing's worth doing, it's worth doing badly? Half measures are best, is that the principle?'

'I think I have divided loyalties.'

'You can't make omelettes without breaking eggs!'

'Don't push me, Ivan. I'm still thinking it through.'

'*Thinking? Ha!*'

'Bully!'

'Wet!'

'Socialist *thug*!'

'Cringing *revisionist*!'

Sophie was reaching out to slap him hard when Tanya, hearing the quarrel through her bedroom door and fearing sudden cancellation of her performance if she delayed, screamed.

A most terrible dream . . .

The scream was such a scream, such a long fierce scream, that all the other sounds of the house dropped into total silence. Then there was just the bang of the dining-room door being flung back hard against the wall, and the thud of Henry's feet as he took the stairs four at a time, and burst past Sophie and Ivan, hardly seeing them, into his younger daughter's room.

'Tanya! What is it, Tanya? *What?*'

Tanya stood, wraithlike, in her best long white nightdress.

'I had a dream,' she told him. 'A most terrible dream . . .' Her hands were spread. Her eyes were glazed. 'I dreamed that I was standing outside a dark prison and all along the prison walls were tiny square windows with iron bars across them and people's thin faces staring out between the bars.' Her shoulders shook. 'And I was searching all the windows to see if I could see my granny, but she wasn't there, until I looked up, and far away, right up in the top corner of the prison wall, practically out of sight, I saw a little old white-haired lady clutching the bars, and I could tell that—'

'*Tsssk! Tanya!*'

Tanya broke off. Natasha had appeared in the doorway.

'*Liar!*'

'Natasha! Don't be so brutal! This poor child's just had the most terrible dream—'

'Tsssk! You are a fool, and she a liar!'

'Come now, Natasha.'

'Come now, yourself, Henry Harris. Open your

eyes. Look at her. *Look* at her. And ask her if she chose to dream this terrible dream of her poor dear granny before or after she had changed into her finest nightdress!'

There was a moment's silence, then:

'Tanya!'

Henry looked at her, now in pure white, when he had chased her off to bed in grubby scarlet diamonds. Tanya tried hard to look coolly back, but with her mother standing there, her hair piled high upon her head, in fierce black from head to toe, taller than tall and far more beautiful than usual, she faltered. Her stubborn face suddenly crumpled.

'Back into bed,' said Henry. 'Go on. Hop back in.'

Natasha swept out, past Ivan and Sophie, across the landing and down the stairs. Swinging the dining-room door back dramatically, she pitched her voice to drown out Tanya's self-abasing howls of misery, and declared:

'Which of us, had we known before, would ever have borne children? I ask you.'

The guests all looked up at Natasha momentarily, then back at the blue-feather-hatted old apparition that, stirred into wakefulness by

Tanya's scream, had just shuffled along in slippers far too large for it, and settled in Natasha's chair.

'The apparition spoke. 'Just what I say. The day I first held Henry in my arms, my own mother said to me: "Adelaide, he's born now. And soon you'll know that when they're young they make your arms ache, but when they're old they make your heart ache".'

Outside the door Henry Harris straightened up the shirt collar that Tanya, in her transports of shame, had pulled around under one ear, half strangling him.

'I'll kill my mother,' Henry was muttering. 'I'll walk in there, walk in and kill her. I will, so help me. I will kill her.'

Peach-and-feather sorbet

Natasha came from a country that knew what real bad times were: failed harvests, men in uniform, barbed wire at snow-covered border posts, night knocks upon the door. She found herself recovering much faster than Henry.

'Adelaide!' she cried. 'Here just in time for heavenly dessert. Find one more chair, Henry. Do help your mother. Take off her hat.'

As Mrs Harris struggled with her hatpins, a shower of blue feathers shimmered through the air and landed on the pretty china dishes heaped high with fresh peach sorbet. Picking one more than usually moth-eaten specimen off his own serving, Henry's headmaster said:

'Have you come very far, Mrs Harris?'

'No distance at all,' Henry's mother assured him. 'The shortest of walks. I can do it in no time.'

'That's wonderful.'

'Quite wonderful.'

'I'm most impressed.'

The chorus was spontaneous. The talk, all at once, was of what a marvel Henry's mother must be, to make her way on foot at eighty-seven through that perplexing labyrinth out there of Bonnington Circles and Crescents and Closes and Drives, in the pitch dark, and still arrive in time for dessert.

Mrs Harris swelled with the appreciation. She spooned up fresh peach sorbet and feathers and tried hard to concentrate as Henry's headmaster warmly and encouragingly compared her capabilities most favourably with those of his own elderly relations. She lost the thread for a moment when her teeth slipped; but when she realized that Henry's headmaster, instead of continuing to detail her own virtues, had, like a vast dam suddenly unblocked, simply taken to abusing his own ageing mother, she let the cold of sorbet on her new teeth block up her ears entirely.

Ivan, outside the door, heard it all; but even at his breakneck scribble he could not get it all down, word for word. He was reduced, by the sheer speed and richness of the anecdotes, to taking only the briefest of notes to flesh out later, more at his leisure.

'... hides the apostle spoons in the flour bin ...'

Ivan scribbled fast.

'... tips all the pills out and puts them into other bottles, treats them like Smarties... phoned up a dozen times that evening... took the thing out of the dustbin again and wore it to the Prizegiving, covered in peelings... and when I got there, through all that

snow and black ice, all that was wrong was that the volume was turned down... and gets through quarts of sherry, don't know how she does it, never seems drunk... they won't deliver to the house any more, simply can't stand the constant scenes... and I've been married to Martha for over twenty-two years now, but will my mother remember Martha's name? No, she will not... the same book in her lap for four years now. What? What's the title? I don't know. The Life of Mary, Queen of Scots, *I believe. I haven't read it. I don't think she has either, to tell you the truth. It's upside down as often as not... found seven wills, seven, and each had a different member of the family cut off without a penny... used to let her eat with us until she took to taking out her dentures and plonking them down on the table, next to her plate... hates the Health Visitor, I do believe she'd climb out of her coffin to punch her... Lists of things in bundles and hides them all over the bungalow. They've taken to calling her The Squirrel on the estate... turned out it wasn't broken at all, she'd just switched it off at the wall plug, by mistake...'*

Spilled, relieved, drained, the flood waters dropped steadily:

> '...been close to killing her at times. I know I shouldn't say it but it's true...a hair's breadth from matricide on several occasions ...looked at the kitchen knife, truly I have, and...shouldn't go on about it really, sure I'm boring you...just can't imagine the sheer strain of it all...'

Henry gazed across the table and into his headmaster's eyes, appalled by the stories he had heard, suffused with admiration for this man who suffered as he suffered, but worse. Natasha leaned on her bare white elbows, contented, watching her guests behind their empty sorbet dishes and little piles of blue feathers, watching in still fascination as Henry's headmaster's deep feeling tirade slowly abated. They'd most of them known Henry's headmaster for years, and never heard him talking like this. No one had ever smashed through that chilly reserve before. But trust it all to happen at Natasha's! Trust that exotic Russian passion to spread around a dinner table as though it were catching! What tales! What guests!

What food! Down to the feathers in the sorbet!

Henry's mother's hearing came back as her new teeth warmed. She looked up hopefully. She'd not refuse another helping of that delicious peach and feather sorbet, but that demented man across the table was still going on and on and on about his poor mother.

If no one else here was capable of stemming the tide, then it was clearly up to her.

'Oh, she does sound a *trial*,' said Mrs Harris. 'But I think I may safely say I've been no trouble to *my* son.'

Henry, transfixed still, answered automatically.

'That's right, Mum. Been no trouble. None at all.'

Almost two-thirty

Sophie lay listening to the party's farewells, still awake, partly out of loyalty because poor Ivan was still filling in the awful details of the headmaster's mother before he forgot them, partly because the light, still on for Ivan, bothered her.

The voices swept up through the house, as gay and lively as six hours ago.

'Wonderful! Don't know when I've enjoyed myself more.'

'Великольгачо, Natasha!'

'Can't *tell* you how much better I feel. Just getting it all off one's chest for once seems to help enormously.'

'Yes. That one's mine. And Alfred's is that mangy duffel coat.'

'Don't think they stock blue feathers yet at Giovanni's.'

'*Une merveille! Quatre-vingt sept ans! Quelle merveille!*'

'Goodnight. Goodnight.'

'Could drop your dear mother off for you in Bonnington Circle. Or was it Bonnington Mews?'

'Goodnight.'

'Спокоріной ночи.'

'Goodnight.'

Sophie unobtrusively slid her hand around the bed's edge and, coughing to disguise the switch's click, turned her electric blanket on again.

'You shouldn't do that,' Ivan reproved her. 'What with my body weight, the blanket might overheat and fuse. Or worse.'

'Get off my bed then. Sit on the floor instead.'

'I've about finished now.'

'Good thing. I'm tired out. It's almost two-thirty.'

'It was worth it.'

'Yes,' Sophie said. 'It obviously went off beautifully. I do believe the headmaster must have been a little drunk. I heard him laughing at the very end. No one has ever stayed this late before. It must have been a stunning success. Well worth all the effort they put into it.'

'I meant for us. Worth it for us.'

'Oh?'

'I have ten, fifteen pages here, Sophie. *Look* at it. Background, examples, social problems. Look at it all.'

He spun the pages past her tired eyes. She pushed him off the bed onto the floor.

'Ivan, you're a fanatic.'

'They've found a
space . . .'

Phone call

Sophie realized it was a phone call about Granny the moment she saw her father hastily shutting himself and the telephone into the shoe cupboard beneath the stairs. She heard him crashing down among the rollerblades and rusty gerbil cages, and then his muffled voice through the wood panels, but she couldn't hear what he was saying. When he stopped talking, she backed away into the kitchen, where Natasha sat, beside the window, silent and expressionless, sipping her tea.

Some moments later, Henry Harris joined them.

'Who called?' Natasha asked.

'School suppliers,' Henry Harris lied. 'Those grammar books for Year Eleven French will be another two weeks coming.'

Natasha looked straight through him, out the other side, and at the wall behind him.

'They found a space for your old mother.'

Henry went red. He thought of rallying, and then better of it.

'Meredith House,' Henry admitted. 'If we phone up, we can go round and have a look.'

'When?'

'At the weekend.'

As she began to rise at once, he added:

'So how about next Saturday?'

'Today is Sunday. Sunday is weekend, too.'

'Today? That's a bit sudden, isn't it?'

'To look,' Natasha reassured him. 'Only to look.'

Pushing her teacup aside, she stretched behind her for the telephone directory and started riffling through the pages.

'T ... P ... M ... Munty ... Morton ... Meredith ... Meredith Samuel ... Meredith House!'

She laid her finger on the place. Her hair fell back as she stood up, excited, galvanized. She looked strange, Sophie thought, until she realized with a shock she simply looked younger.

'Natasha ... Not so fast, please. Natasha! At least drink up your tea first. *Please.*'

'My tea?'

Natasha drew back from him, letting loose that half of the directory her hand was holding down. The pages whipped across, a sudden vicious fan, back into place.

'Tea? Tea? Чаз – не дрова руочть,' she snarled, and left the room. The door's slam shook the room. Small crumblings of plaster slithered down the wall in the corner.

Sophie was horrified.

'What did she say?' she asked her father. 'What did she say just then? What *was* that she just said? *Daddy?*'

Henry reached out for the directory and started leafing through.

'She's right,' he said. 'She's quite right, really. She said, "To sip tea isn't to hew wood", and she's quite right. Meredith House. Here we are. Here's the number. She's quite right.'

Bossy bitch

'Please move back, Gran,' Sophie said again. 'Your legs are scorching. I can see them scorching.'

Her grandmother kept her arms stubbornly folded, ignoring her.

'Please, Gran.'

No move. Nothing at all.

'Then let me just pull your armchair back from the fire a little.'

'Don't touch my chair! I've got it how I like it! You leave it!'

'Oh, *Gran.*'

Sophie felt tired out and close to tears. There was no one around to help. The others were all on their way to Meredith House by now. She had to handle this by herself.

'Gran, *please.* Your legs are *burning.*'

She stepped behind the huge armchair, and tugged. The dead weight of it on the thick rug made her task hopeless and she knew it.

'Please, Gran. Oh, *please.*'

She'd never seen her grandmother in this

mood before. Perhaps it was last night's late night, or the rich food, or both.

She tugged at the heavy armchair again.

'Gran!'

'Don't touch my chair, you bossy bitch!'

Sophie stepped back, shocked.

'I'll turn the fire off, then,' she said. 'I will. I'll *have* to. If you won't help me move your chair back, I'll have to turn the fire right off.'

'Don't you dictate to me, young madam! Who do you think you are anyway? Are you a nurse? I'm bloody glad I'm not one of *your* patients!'

'Gran! This is Sophie. Sophie! Gran?'

'You're just a bossy little madam, that's what you are. I suppose you're one of that Natasha's daughters. Or one of Henry's.'

'Gran, please move back. *Please!*'

Sophie gazed round the room in desperation. Her eyes fell on a thick shawl tossed across the bed. She fetched it, and praying that the old lady wouldn't start up all over again, came up and tried to tuck it in over the old skirt, so that it fell in folds over the reddening shins.

Mrs Harris clucked and hissed at her crossly. She slapped out, feeble little slaps, at Sophie's busy hands. Sophie was stronger. Mrs Harris failed to prise the thick shawl off, and by the time Sophie stepped hastily back out of sight behind the chair, she seemed to have forgotten who had put it there, or why, and laid her hands down in her lap again.

Sophie stood, perfectly still, behind the armchair and the nodding head, until she felt quite sure the battle was entirely forgotten.

Horrid old woman, she was thinking. Nasty, ungrateful old cow. She bloody well *deserves* to go in a Home.

You know . . .

The road to Meredith House went round the common, where there were roadworks. The men were leaning on their equipment, idle. A huge articulated lorry was temporarily blocking both lanes. The woman who held the Stop/Go sign leaned it against the side of a tar lorry, showing the Stop sign. Exhaust stopped rising from the rear of the car in front of him, so Henry Harris turned his engine off as well, and rolled the window down. A blast of cold air swept him on one side, blasts of abuse from every other.

'Tsssk!'

'Dad-*dee*!'

'I'm *cold*!'

'That draught is frightful in the back, you know.'

Henry rolled up the window again. The deeps of his mind registered that he was one familiar complainant short. He said:

'I hope Sophie's all right.'

'Sophie will cope.'

'We've never left her responsible for Mother for so long before.'

'So what can happen?'

Henry, cross with Natasha, hating the trip, said:

'She might just *die* on Sophie, that's all.'

Natasha turned her head away and looked across the bleak grey common.

'Your mother will outlive us all,' she said.

The workmen lit up cigarettes. Ivan looked round for signs that said Inflammable. Tanya and Nicholas fought surreptitiously for room. The longer that the car sat stationary, the more the clamour in the back seat built up.

'*Where* are we going? What's the place called?'

'How far is it? Are we nearly there?'

'How old is Granny, anyway? Is Granny *really* eighty-seven?'

'How come she's eighty-seven?'

'Yes. How come Granny is so *old*?'

'She took her time,' said Henry.

'I *mean*,' insisted Tanya. '*If* you're only forty-two, which you *claim*, then Granny must have been forty-five years old already when she had you. And Mummy's not that old yet and she's had four of us and how come *that*, that's what I mean.'

'Yes. How come *that*?'

Henry gave it a bit of thought. It was some years since he'd considered it.

'Your grandmother married rather late.'

'*Rather* late!'

'*Why*?'

'Maybe she didn't find the right man.'

'Maybe there were no men to find,' said Natasha. 'Where I grew up there have been times when there were fewer men than wolves.'

'I don't think healthy young men were all that thick on the ground round here after the First World War, either,' Henry said tartly.

Tanya and Nicholas, sensing the quarrel on its way, stopped kicking one another.

Then Ivan said:

'It wasn't that, you know.'

'What?' Henry drummed the steering wheel with his fingers. 'It wasn't what?'

'What you two said. About there being no one around for Granny to marry. It wasn't that. It was a personal thing.'

'Personal?'

'A misunderstanding,' Ivan explained. 'Just a mistake. And what with both her parents being so strict, and living on that farm away from art galleries and so forth, and there not being television or anyone around for her to talk to, she just didn't realize for years and years.'

'She didn't realize *what*?'

'Her mistake. You see, she thought she was the only woman in the world who had thick curly hairs in her armpits and down—' Seeing his father's eyes on him through the mirror and quite misunderstanding the appalled expression, he changed what he was going to say to: 'Well, you know . . .'

Natasha slid round in her seat and quelled Tanya's nervous giggle with one short look. She searched her elder son's face hard for one relieving sign that he might be lying.

'You made that up! Ivan!'

Ivan was pale but firm. He shook his head.

'Who told you?'

'Sophie.'

Sophie never lied. The family sat in total silence, knowing that Sophie, back at the house with her grandmother, never lied.

Henry stopped drumming, gripped the steering wheel. He stared ahead at the grey misted-over windscreen as though he were driving. Natasha rolled her window down. This time not one of them complained about the cold. Through the small mirror Ivan watched the tears roll down his father's face and wondered what would happen when the road cleared.

It was some time before the workwoman reached for her sign and, as the huge articulated lorry pulled in fitful jerks across to the side, spun it around to Go. Natasha opened her door, stepped out and swung it closed behind her. She walked round the car and, as her husband slid across the seat, slipped in his place and started up the engine.

Although the workwoman stubbornly held the sign displaying Go, the line of cars drawn up behind was forced to wait a little longer. Natasha blocked both lanes, turning with neither signals nor the slightest regard for other vehicles, turning and driving back the way they had come, away from Meredith House, towards home, the children still and silent in the back, her husband shaking, wet-faced, at her side.

'I only said...'

'You made him cry.'
  'He cried, yes. I didn't make him.'
'You made him cry.'
'Sophie, I only said to him what you once told me.'
'You made him cry.'
'Sophie, you're being quite ridiculous—'
'I hate you, Ivan. I *hate* you.'
'Sophie!'

Sophie thinks about it

Sophie checked through the bright yellow note-book to see if there was any other work of her own hidden in there that she should rescue before she handed the Granny Project over to Ivan for him to finish as he chose, alone. One passage after another caught her eye, slowing her up, making her think.

Mr H said that the worst thing about having an old person in the house was being trapped in evening after evening in case of fires, and day after day because of meals, without even the compensation that you have with children of knowing roughly how long your prison sentence is going to last. Mrs H was then heard to mutter something in a foreign tongue, later translated as: Young ones get better; old ones get worse.

Mr H said: She makes me feel as old as she is. Older! She's in her second childhood, after all.

Mrs H looked exhausted by lunchtime, but the discussion about the possibility of getting a new, larger tumble dryer was postponed, apparently in the vague hope that the problem would go away.

Mr H was heard to scream: 'I'll talk to her. All right. As it's her birthday, I will go and talk to her. If she would only ramble on pleasantly about how her mother churned butter by hand in the old days on the farm in Furlay, I'd go and talk to her every night! I'd enjoy it. But she's not interested in any of that. That's all dead and gone. She'll want to talk about Fairways, or Solomon Street, or what they did tonight on Classroom Clangers. Oh, yes. I'll go and talk to her, since she's my mother and it's her birthday. But when I cut my throat, you'll all know why.'

Mr H said: 'I've found a use for her at last. We'll prop her up in the front window to frighten off the Jehovah's Witnesses.'

Mrs H said: 'One Novosibirsk winter, that is all it takes . . .'

Mr H plucked several feathers out of the hat, and threw it on the floor and stamped on it.

Mr H finally agreed to get a wreath for Harry Rowe who was not dead yet. He climbed back in his house through a small window in the kitchen, later found to be cracked.

The H family have not been on any holidays for eight years now, not even a weekend.

Mrs H said that if the public library reading room, five minutes' walk away, did not exist, she would not choose to either.

Mrs H said: 'She will outlive us all.'

Sophie closed the notebook and put it away in a drawer, out of sight. She went down to the kitchen, where Natasha sat at the table, peeling parsnips, humming. Sophie sat opposite. She dipped her fingers in the bowl of clear water, spinning the parsnips round and round in it, and asked:

'What if there are absolutely overwhelming

reasons for doing something, and, when you think about it, just as overwhelming reasons for doing just the opposite?'

Natasha considered.

'You could think longer.'

'No, it's not that. The more you think, the more you get to want to choose both ways.'

'So you could wait.'

'What for?'

'For things to change?'

'What if they don't change?'

'Accept the situation? Do nothing?' Seeing the look on Sophie's face, she added: 'But I see you are still too young for that. So then, you could forget about it.' And when the look came back again. 'No. I can see that you are now too old for that. So.'

'So?'

'So I can't help you.'

'No one can?'

'No.'

'Ivan, you know, can just block out one side.'

'Ivan was single-minded from the womb.'

'Unfeeling, I call it.'

'He will go far.'

'Go far! Ivan will end up as a hijacker or something. Or else some cold and merciless revolutionary, leaving his wife and children to go off to kill complete strangers for some lofty principle.'

'Sophie—'

'Liquidating all those with different priorities, hurling his bombs—'

'Sophie!'

'Plotting in cells—'

'*Sophie!*'

'And *dying* in a cell! Shot in the head, splattered, a broken egg in one of his own bloody omelettes!'

Natasha said, picking her words with care:

'There are all sorts of people in the world. You are one sort and Ivan is another.'

'My sort is better. My sort is *kinder.*'

'Ivan might say: You kind people can distribute free sacks of grain to scores of starving peasants, but I am here across the same valley, planning the revolution that will give them back their land.'

'And getting thousands killed while he does it!'

'Dying of wounds, dying of hunger – dying is the same.'

'You think he's *right?*'

'I'm not sure that he's wrong.'

'You know about what happened to your own Revolution!'

'I also know about the way things were before.'

'Right or not, I don't have to like or respect him.'

'A revolutionary is never liked or respected. It's worship or hate, depending on which side you're on.'

'I don't know yet which side I'm on. That's just what I've been *telling* you.'

She slammed out of the room so fast, she didn't hear Natasha saying:

'And I was listening. I heard.'

Чем яапьше ьдес , мем яодьше

Henry knocked twice on Sophie's door and as she failed to shout Go Away at him, took this to be an invitation, and walked on in. In one hand he was carrying a small rectangular piece of white card, and in the other tacks and a hammer.

Sophie sat upright on the bed, rubbing the tear-marks off her cheeks. 'What do you want?'

'I've brought you this.'

'What?'

'This.'

Henry held out a piece of card. He came a little closer to the bed, so she could see the fine Russian lettering on it.

'What's that, then? Not another *proverb*!'

Henry looked round the room.

'I think it would look rather nice on that wall there.'

'Well, I don't want it.'

'Shall I just take it down to her again?'

'Yes! No . . .' The lettering was beautiful. It clearly had been done with great care. 'Oh, I don't know. Depends what it *says*.'

'It says,' and Henry read aloud in his best accent:

'Чем дальше в лес, тем ъолдшы дпов.'

'Oh, well,' said Sophie sarcastically. 'Naturally, in that case, I'd *love* it.'

Henry made a performance of choosing just the right spot on the wall. He danced from left to right, held up the card, stepped back and forward, frowning and pondering. Only when Sophie finally smiled for him did he actually push the tack through the thin card and bang it in the wall.

He stepped back to admire his handiwork, and Sophie said:

'What does it *mean*, then? Since it's up there now.'

'It means: The further into the wood you go, the more trees you will find.'

'Oh, yes?'

'Good proverb, that, Sophie. Solid. Deep. It's satisfying. Not like some of them. A good proverb, that one.'

'Oh, yes?'

'Yes.'

'What did she send it up to *me* for?'

Henry picked up his hammer, ready to go.

'I expect she thought you needed it,' he said.

Paresthesia

'What we have here,' the doctor confided, 'is simply lumbar osteoarthritis compressing nerve roots, with this resultant paresthesia.'

'Oh, yes?' Henry looked hopeful. 'It's paresthesia she's got now, is it?'

The family sat around the kitchen table, taking this in. Natasha asked: 'What's paresthesia?' and when she heard the doctor clear his throat she added hastily:

'Just in a word.'

'Briefly, for the layman,' Henry backed her up.

'The typical man in the street,' put in Ivan.

'Your common or garden punter,' said Sophie.

'Mr Average,' Tanya said.

'The general—'

'*Tssk!*'

Natasha's fierce hiss quashed Nicholas's contribution instantly. They all turned back to look at the doctor, who said:

'Jumpy legs.'

'I beg your pardon?' Henry Harris said.

'Jumpy legs. Her paresthesia. In this case it's what your average chap would call jumpy legs.'

Natasha glowered at Henry.

'You have it, too,' she accused him. 'You'll no doubt go the way your mother's gone. This paresthesia is, I expect, some Harris family curse.'

'An insignificant genetic flaw, perhaps,' Henry fought back.

'Like haemophilia,' Tanya led off the family chorus.

'Or muscular dystrophy.'

'Or sickle cell anaemia.'

'Or Tay Sachs syndrome.'

'Or—'

'*Tsssk!*'

The doctor stood up, buttoning his coat.

'Least of her problems, anyway,' he said. 'And the whole thing will be off your hands within a few days. They'll let you know what time to bring her in, and what she's to take.'

As he walked down the hall towards the front door, followed by Henry, they heard his phrases floating back at them: '...inflammation of the synovial membrane...ankylosis of ligaments... atrophy of contiguous muscle...proximal inter-phalangeal joints...' and Henry's plaintive echoes: '...can hardly make it to the bathroom now...stiff as a board, she all but *creaks*...all swollen up, poor soul...sits still for more than twenty minutes, she sort of *sets*...mistook me for some long-gone great-uncle of hers this morning...'

Natasha circled round the kitchen, like a bat, fast and tense. The children watched her. At one point, lifting up her head, she noticed them, and then the way that they were watching her.

'You!' she cried, pointing a thin finger. 'You! When you have laid me and your father kindly and safely in *our* graves, then you may look at me as you do now. Only then!'

Hateful quarrelling

Tanya had quite a temper when she let herself go, and she was letting herself go. Her voice echoed shrilly against the metal sheet of garage door which Nicholas had pulled down for privacy as soon as he saw the way the meeting was going.

'Taken the whole thing over!' she was shouting. 'It was supposed to be the four of us. Nicholas and I did our best with the nightmares, and since you called those off, we haven't been able to do another thing for this project. You haven't thought of anything else for us at all. You haven't even tried! It isn't fair. It wasn't our fault that Natasha saw through that nightmare business so quickly—'

'It *was* your fault,' Ivan interrupted. 'It was that fancy nightdress of yours she saw through.'

'It was a see-through nightdress!' Nicholas crowed.

Tanya spun on him, pointing like her mother.

'You! You can laugh. You two can laugh. But it's not *fair*! Sophie backs out of the whole project of her own accord. Then Ivan goes off and works on it in secret, day after day. I've seen that yellow notebook, Ivan. I've looked at it. It's all filled up. You've done about a hundred pages, I should think! You've got the whole of the last month written up in there! What Granny says. What Daddy says to Granny. What Mum and Dad say about Granny behind her back. The lot! And do you know what he's got in the back? Charts! Charts and appendices! Appendices and charts on *everything*. What Granny eats. What Granny wears. What Granny drinks. What time they put her into bed each night. He's even got a chart on what percentage of the laundry piles is Granny's stuff! He heard Natasha complaining that ninety per cent of every washload was Granny's wet sheets, and now he's sorting every load out secretly, and weighing them.'

'You're not,' said Sophie. 'Are you?'

'None of your business,' Ivan snapped at her. 'You're out of this whole project now.

You're only at this meeting on sufferance.'

'Because you can't throw me out!' Sophie jeered.

'Because I can't throw you out.'

'Ivan, I've told you this before. You're a fanatic.' Tanya kicked at the tea chest they were sitting on.

'There! Off you go again. Ivan! Ivan! Ivan! I'm talking about *me*! Me and Nicholas! What do *we* get to do! Nothing! Granny is going into Meredith House on Monday morning, and now we're talking about *him* again. Oh, Sophie, make him think up something good for Nicholas and me to do.'

Nicholas said:

'I don't want anything to do. I'm dropping out, like Sophie. I don't care any longer where Granny goes. I just can't stand any more of all this hateful quarrelling.'

'That's just what Mum and Dad say!'

'Maybe they're *right*, then.'

Tanya shrieked at him:

'You don't love Granny. That's what it is, you know. You don't love Granny!'

'Oh, shut up, Tanya!' Sophie said.

'Don't tell me to shut up. Shut up yourself!'

'I've hardly spoken! None of us has! This whole

meeting has just been you, flouncing around peeved out of your selfish tiny mind because you haven't got the star part in this farce.'

'*Farce?* Oh, I see! She's not just spinelessly backed out on us. Her priggish Majesty has also decided this is a *farce*.'

'It *is* a farce. This whole thing is a farce. A pretty nasty one, too, I think. That Social Science project is due in on Monday morning, first thing. Ivan will hand in his Granny Project and get himself a shining A Star, I'm sure. Ivan will be all right, you'll see. But Dad won't.'

She turned away from Tanya. She turned on Ivan.

'Dad won't lift up his head again in the staffroom, once everything that's in that Granny Project gets about. The other teachers will all read it, you can be sure of that. They'll all pretend they haven't, but they will. Miss Ballantyne will probably show enough sensitivity to "lose" it before the end of term display of work, but they'll all have read it. It will get about. And then somebody, anybody, just someone a bit more spiteful and daring than all the others, will ask Dad, oh, so casually, in between classes: "How's your old mother, Henry?" And then he'll know everyone has read it. And when he comes home, close to tears, and looks at Ivan, Ivan will look right back at him, won't you? You'll look right back at him and preach about not being able to make omelettes without breaking eggs!'

'It isn't going to work out that way, stupid.'

'What makes you quite so sure of that?'

'Because it's all planned out, that's why. No one at school will ever see the project.'

'No?'

'No! *Listen.* I leave the finished project on the kitchen table. Natasha doesn't even notice it's there—'

'Good thing, or she would slap your face.'

'Natasha doesn't notice it. But Henry does. He picks it up to see how my school work is going, and once he realizes what he's just found, he reads the whole thing, end to end—'

'And punches out your lights for you.'

'And shows it to Natasha. She reads it too. They talk it over in bed that night, and in the morning he approaches me and asks me for an explanation.'

'And smashes in your ugly face!'

'And so what, Sophie, if he does? The Granny Project still exists.'

Sophie laughed scornfully.

'He'll rip it up.'

'And I have copies.'

'Oh.'

There was a silence. Then:

'You've thought it all out, haven't you?'

'Of course I have. There's no point, otherwise.'

'I feel *ill* when I think all this grew out of my idea.'

'It's going to work out, Sophie. Believe me. Listen. He'll ask me what the whole thing is about. I'll tell him. He'll express strong doubts about the wisdom of giving such a personal thing in at the school where he teaches. He'll talk to me about family solidarity—'

'Family *feeling*.'

'What?'

'*Feeling*, Ivan. The word is family *feeling*. Or family *loyalty*. Either. But not solidarity. You want to watch it, Ivan. You're starting to get all those woolly ideological words confused with real life!'

'Well, family feeling, then. Whatever it is, he'll talk about it. Then I will lead a counter-attack. I'll talk about our fears about Granny. They'll talk about how rotten Dad will feel if my great project goes to school. I'll talk about how rotten we'll feel if Granny goes into that Home.'

'You'll threaten them.'

'It's called negotiation, Sophie.'

'It's called intimidation.'

'I call it working for a viable compromise.'

'I call it *blackmail*.'

'Well, call it what you want. At least it is a plan, and one that more than likely will work.'

'Like kidnapping your enemy's children. Or ripping people's fingernails out to get the information you want.'

In the dim light of the closed garage, Nicholas's face glimmered with horror.

'They don't do that, do they?'

'They do,' said Sophie. 'Oh, yes they do. People with noble ideas and no feelings, like Ivan here.'

Ivan hit Sophie. He hit her good and hard on the face with his clenched fist. His curled-up knuckles caught the ridge of bone above her eye. The pain was intense. She dropped her head between her knees and pushed her palm against the pain, harder and harder, trying to block it off, flatten the sharpness of it in her brain.

Tanya flew at her brother. Pinching a fold of skin on his arm between her fingers, she twisted it hard, and dug her fingernails well in for good measure. Bright tears of pain sprang into Ivan's eyes. He slapped her face with his free hand and Tanya stumbled backwards, shocked off balance, onto Nicholas, scraping his ankle badly.

Nobody moved. All four of them were struggling with tears.

'Is it a joke?'

A coffee break

Henry picked up the yellow notebook that was lying on the kitchen table. The title was intriguing. *The Granny Project, by Ivan Harris. For Social Science.* It sounded impressive. He flicked it open to see how well his son was getting on these days in another school subject. He was surprised to see how much there was of it, almost a whole book, over ninety pages, closely written.

A calculation of the exact number of hours that her fire was actually on in one typical winter week gives the lie to the frequently expressed claim by Mr H. that 'If it weren't for her and her multi-kilowatt gobbling fire, I reckon all our heating bills would be a quarter of what they are.' In fact, as the chart Electrical Consumption in Appendix 14 shows (see p. 77) . . .

> *Mr and Mrs H seemed almost disappointed*
> *to hear that paresthesia (jumpy legs) was not*
> *a fatal disease . . .*

Henry closed up the yellow notebook and laid it back upon the table. He stared at it for a moment, thinking. Then he quite slowly and deliberately prepared himself a large mug of coffee. He took down from the cupboard over the sink a packet of his favourite biscuits, and set them, with the coffee, on a small tray. He put the yellow notebook on the tray, and carried it out of the kitchen along to his mother's room, where he knew he could read it through, quite undisturbed by children.

Ivan!

'*I*van!'
   The bellow shook the house.
'IVAN!'
Ivan closed up the book that he'd been trying to read and laid it on the bed beside Sophie. He

hoped, by putting it down right beside her, to prompt her into looking up and speaking to him, and she did.

'Well, good luck, anyway.'

'Thank you.'

The skin round her left eye was purple today, and that side of her face was badly swollen.

'It sounds as if you're going to need it,' Tanya said.

'Thank you.'

'We could come down, too,' Nicholas offered.

'No. Thank you.'

Well ...

Henry was standing waiting for his son in the kitchen. When Ivan closed the door behind him and turned to face his father, he saw the yellow notebook lying on the table between them like Exhibit A in a trial.

'This thing here,' said Henry. 'This – Granny Project. Well ...?'

'Yes?'

'*I'm* asking *you*.'

Ivan was startled by the tone of voice, the cold and absolute hostility. Trying to keep from sounding insolent, for he could sense how thin the ice was he was stepping on, he said:

'Asking me what?'

Henry laid each hand flat upon the kitchen table, one either side of the notebook. He leaned his weight a little forward and Ivan saw, just from the way his father stood there, as if he were in school behind his desk, that he had slipped into that other side of him, the side that Ivan's schoolfriends saw of him, and that he could no longer be relied on to be like Henry when he was at home.

'Just what did you intend to do with this?'

'Well . . . It's due in on Monday, actually.'

'Is it a joke?'

'A joke?'

'I see. Not a joke.'

'No.'

'You chose this topic?'

'Yes. Well. It was Sophie's idea at the start.'

'I don't see Sophie's name on this.' He picked the notebook up and peered at it, sarcastic teacher fashion, searching for Sophie's name, which wasn't there. Ivan felt angry. It was, he thought, an unfair trespass on their own relationship, this sudden acting like a form-master. He said, very coldly:

'Sophie dropped out some time ago.'

'Sophie thought better of it all, perhaps?'

Ivan fought rising panic. This interview, which he'd gone over time and again in his mind, was getting out of hand. He had, he realized, always planned it with himself in control, raising the issues, guiding the discussion. It wasn't going that way at all. His father was attempting to sidetrack him with tricks, petty school tricks, to make him feel small and angry. So keep calm, keep thinking. Don't let these messy feelings in. Feelings confuse. Keep thinking, thinking.

'Sophie did change her mind, yes.'

'And so you finished it. Alone.'

'Yes.'

'All your own work.'

'Yes. Mostly.'

'Why?'

'Why? Well, for Social Science.'

'Please don't prevaricate. I'll ask you one more time. Why did you do it?' He was really angry now.

Ivan stood, silent. He heard the words he'd

used to justify the project ring in his ears – negotiation, working towards a viable compromise, legitimate aim. And then he heard in Sophie's clear uncompromising voice her own, more brutal, version of what he was about: threats and intimidation, *blackmail*. To Ivan, suddenly, Sophie's words seemed more real; his own feeble, evasive, meaningless.

Ivan had pride and he was honest. He looked straight at his father and said:

'It is supposed to be a kind of blackmail.'

'I see.'

'To stop you putting Granny in that Home.'

'We keep your Granny here or you will hand this in at school?'

'That's right.'

'I see.'

Henry paced up and down the kitchen, as if he might be thinking it out. From time to time he shot quick looks at Ivan, who stood, quite expressionless, watching him.

Henry stopped at the window.

'Tell me,' he said. 'In the event that I should knuckle under, were you prepared to go into school empty-handed tomorrow and get a failing mark for not having a shred of work to show? Or have you some back-up project on a less contentious subject safely written up?'

'Of course not!'

'You sound surprised that I should ask.'

'Well . . . That would be – dishonourable.'

'And this?' Henry swooped on the notebook suddenly and rapped it with his knuckles, hard. 'This thing. This vicious and disloyal document. This hurtful and insensitive piece of trash. This catalogue of eavesdroppings. You don't feel this to be dishonourable?'

'I *feel* it is, yes. Yes, I do,' Ivan admitted. 'But I don't *think* it is. With Sophie, all the feelings took over. That's why she dropped out halfway through. I reconsidered at that time. Of course I did. But I still thought that I was right, so I kept going.'

'Christ, Ivan.'

His father sat down heavily at the table.

'Ivan, you're a fanatic. You know that.'

'Sophie says that.'

'I don't know.' Henry put his head in his hands. 'I don't know, Ivan. Truly I don't. The idea of a son of mine acting like this, thinking this through in such a cold, inhuman fashion. It makes my blood run cold, you know that? You carry on this way, without a hint of sympathy or imagination or warmth, and God knows what a warped and barbarous mess you'll make of your life. God knows where you'll end up.'

'Sophie thinks I'll end up in some prison for revolutionaries.'

'Christ, Ivan! What a waste and failure!'

'I don't see why.'

'You can't *do* anything in prison. You simply sit there, wasting out your life. That is the point of it. If you want to change things, try to improve things a bit, have a purpose, you have to stay out here with the rest of us!'

He saw his son's face set into stubbornness.

'Oh, never mind,' he said. 'Off you go.'

'Go?'

'Yes. Go away. Go and find Sophie. If you can persuade her to give you a hand, you should be able to hash up some apology for a Social Science project by Monday morning. You've got a lot of odd statistics here. Go and knit them into something else. Sophie and you can think of something between you, I'm sure.'

Ivan had pride and honesty, and he had courage too.

'I'm giving in the Granny Project at school on

Monday,' he said. 'Unless you promise me that you will keep her here. That's what I wrote it for. I've worked very hard. I have a purpose I believe in. That's not changed. You're hurt and angry with me, but I knew you'd be hurt and angry. I took all that into account right from the start, and still I carried on. There is no point in backing down now. If you can't see I've taken everything into account, you must think I've been playing games. I haven't. You can throw that notebook there over a cliff, but I have copies—'

'Ivan, I do believe I'd like to beat you up!'

'It wouldn't help.'

'I would feel better.'

'Feelings!'

At the jibe, Henry's hand clenched into a fist. He might have been tempted to put the fist in Ivan's face, but that the memory of poor Sophie's eye, the swelling and discolour and sheer ugliness of bruising, was still too fresh and real for him to close his mind to the sure consequence. Instead, he said:

'Get out! Get out of here! Get *out!*'

And Ivan left, as calmly and deliberately as he had come in.

Лео оьь Не Кармошка, Не
ьыьпосмшь ь окошко

(Love is not a potato: you cannot throw it out of the window)

Natasha sat on the bed and peeled her tights off.

'It chills my bones. A blackmailer in my own family. My first-born son. My blood and bone. Of all the crimes! He should be something useful, like a poisoner, and practise on his granny.'

'I could just beat him up, Natasha. I'd enjoy that.'

'You hold him. I will beat him up.'

'We could throw him out of the house. By his behaviour he's forfeited all rights to be a member of this family. How old is he? What's the law? Is he old enough to be thrown out?'

'Люшовь не карторка,' Natasha said. ' Не сышрос, ыші в окошйо.'

'I never heard that one before,' said Henry.

'I never had sad cause to say it before.'

She draped her underwear over the bedstead.

'Listen, my darling,' she told him. 'I have a plan . . .'

Bonfire

On Sunday evening Henry went in search of Ivan. He told him that, after giving everything more thought, Natasha and he had decided Granny should stay. Ivan stood by as Henry phoned up Meredith House to tell them of the sudden change of plan. When Henry had put down the telephone, Ivan put in his hands the yellow notebook, and all the photocopies he had made.

He was astonished when his father thanked him cheerfully and patted him on the back.

Henry went out into the dark and lit a small bonfire by the compost heap. He burned the lot.

Ivan stood well back in the shadows of the bushes, feeling unaccountably disturbed. He watched the roughly torn up remains of all his hours of work float up in pretty orange splutters, then melt into the black overhead. He didn't for a moment believe his father would renege on their agreement; but still he felt deeply uneasy.

Henry watched over the fire till the very end, enthusiastically prodding the shrinking body of it with a long stick. From start to finish he kept up a solid and high-spirited whistling.

F

'You haven't anything to show me, Ivan?'
'Nothing.'
'No notes, even? Something not yet written up?'
'No.'
'A list of books you've read?'
'No. I'm afraid not.'
'This project, you know, counts for half a term's marks.'
'I know it does.'
'So may I have an explanation?'
'I'm sorry.'
'Sorry is not an explanation.'
'Sorry.'
'F, then. It's all that I can do. I'm sorry.'
'That's all right.'
'Right . . . F, then. I'm sorry.'
'It's quite all right, Miss Ballantyne. Honestly.'
'Well . . . F, then. Sorry.'

'Some might have called it blackmail.'

Checkmate

When Natasha made the formal announcement over supper that Granny wouldn't be going into the Home after all, Tanya and Nicholas made little faces of triumph and congratulation across the table at Ivan. Ivan, still smarting from his first Fail ever, gave them a small nod back and turned to Sophie for her approbation. He had, after all, achieved their object for them, and surely Sophie still approved the end, if not the means.

But Sophie wasn't looking at him. She was still listening to Natasha. Natasha was saying:

'... can see things more clearly through another man's eyes. Some might have called it blackmail. But I prefer to think it was my dear son's only way of letting us know how very strongly he feels about his dear granny's well-being.'

She smiled at Ivan across the dishes, a smile of sheer merry malice.

That most disquieting feeling Ivan had hearing his father's cheery whistle over the bonfire swept back again. Had they a plan? Was that why they both seemed so exhilarated, so united? They sat together at the end of the table like partners in a card game for high stakes who had sleeves full of aces.

'Ivan has made his own position clear. His granny must be cared for in this house. Right?'

She looked at Ivan, eyebrows raised. He sensed a trap, but not what trap. He nodded.

'Fine. Very well,' she said. 'It is agreed. Your grandmother will stay living here. And Ivan will look after her.'

'What?'

'Ivan?'

'By *himself*?'

'*Me*?'

Natasha graciously waved both her hands in the air. 'Ivan, Sophie, Tanya, Nicholas. I do not mind who does what, or who doesn't. The cleaning, shopping, feeding, cup fetching and television channel changing, the bed stripping and laundering and cleaning the lavatory she uses, the

medicine giving and escorting her to the bathroom, mending her clothes, keeping track of her
pension, buying her peppermints, filling her hot
water-bottles, listening to her worries, arranging
the doctor's visits, being here with her after
school and in the evenings and weekends and
holidays, keeping her room warm, switching her
lamps on when it gets dark, tuning her radio,
plumping her pillows, checking she has water
in her water glass' – the hands danced merrily
over the dishes – 'looking for her spectacles,
finding her book, picking up her woollies,
opening her window, closing her window, drawing her curtains, sending her last few Christmas
cards each December, consoling her when her
friends die, reminding her to eat—'

She reeled them off as if they were small
nothings, as if they took no time at all, as if they
hadn't used up half her own life for several
years.

'Do as you choose between you, or leave it all
to Ivan. I don't mind. I have done. Ivan can
arrange it.'

Ivan stared at her.

Sophie said:

'What? *All* of it? *Everything*?'

'Everything. Everything that your father and I have done until now.'

'What about you? What will you do?'

'We will take over your jobs, of course.'

'What jobs?' asked Nicholas, mystified.

'Oh, you know,' said Natasha, airily. 'To pop into her room from time to time, whenever the other television is acting up. To *worry* about the idea of her going into a Home. Henry will have the occasional nightmare on his mother's behalf. I need my sleep, so I will dust around her china ornaments on the dresser on Saturday mornings. I think that sums up what you four have done for her. Have I missed anything?'

'You're joking,' Tanya said. 'You must be.'

'*Not joking!*' The hand came down on the table like a thunderbolt. The dishes jumped. The children's hearts stopped. '*I-am-not-joking!*'

'But—'

'No buts! No buts. No ifs. No backslidings. Upon the first grumble that I hear, she goes or I go.'

'*You* go?'

'You? Go *away*? *Where?*'

'*Where?*'

'Where? Where? I should tell you? No, thank

you. Believe me, I shall get a flat. I will tell Henry where it is. Henry will come and see me there, in peace and quiet.'

'You can't *do* that.'

'I can. I can. I lived like that for years before I had baby Ivan, and I can live like that again. Free from you all, I will be able to work again.' She glowered round the table at each one of them, a beautiful and threatening witch. 'After these years of constant toil, I shall enjoy mere work.'

They all fell quiet. They believed her at last.

Ivan spoke first.

'Blackmail,' he said, and burst out laughing. 'Checkmate! Congratulations!'

She stretched her hand to him across the table. He took it and, for the first time in his life, leaned over and kissed it.

'My blood and bone,' she said. 'You will go far.'

Call Ivan

Natasha floated into Henry's mother's room on air. Her heels were inches high, her skirts shimmered around her as she moved, her bracelets jangled and her earrings flashed. The tiny gold and silver swirls of embroidery on her bodice glinted. Her eyes shone bright.

'Look at you!' Henry's mother said. 'You've got your buttons all sewn on tonight!'

'We're going dancing now,' Natasha announced.

'Dancing? Out dancing? You and my Henry? Fancy!'

Henry came in, easing the collar of his brand new French suit around his brand new brilliant scarlet shirt.

'Oh, Henry!' Mrs Harris cried. 'You look quite foreign!'

'We're off dancing now, Mum,' Henry said.

'Well, look at you! Look at you both! Natasha, you certainly are the permanent flapper!'

Natasha spun her skirts round one last time, planted a kiss on the old lady's cheek, and left on Henry's arm.

'Well!' Mrs Harris told the BBC newsreader. 'Well, *fancy!*'

Natasha poked her head back round the door.

'If there is anything you need,' she said, '*anything*. Call Ivan.'

Carrying the dead cockerel home

Ivan carried in the small wooden supper tray on which he'd put the boiled egg, the buttered toast and the tea. He pushed the cat off Mrs Harris's lap and laid the tray there in its place. Then he perched on the footstool right in front of her to watch her eat it.

'You make a very poor window, young man,' said Mrs Harris. 'I can't see anything but you.'

'What's wrong with me?'

'Nothing. You could charm ducks off water, I'm sure; but I was watching the wedding.'

'What wedding?'

'Behind you. On the telly.'

Ivan swivelled round and, sure enough, behind him on the television screen a lavish wedding scene was unfolding. The bride trembled prettily as one bridesmaid after another darted up to her and, shaking folds of veil into place, whispered sweet, private and encouraging things in her ear. The bridegroom tugged at his stiff cuffs and nervously frowned at his best man. The church was filling up with enormous hats.

'The colour's *awful*. Everything's green.'

'Lay off. Leave them alone. They're all right. Don't you go meddling.'

'The bride's green, too.'

'She's not. She's beautiful.'

'She's *green*. They're all green.'

'Tom Handley is. He's that one glowering behind that pillar. He's wanted to marry Angela for years. He's green with envy that this Marcus got her.'

'Marcus is green too. Everyone's green.'

Ignoring Mrs Harris's expostulations, Ivan fiddled with the colour control until the bride's dress slid from pallid grass colour into brilliant white, her cheeks flushed rosy pink, and all the grapes around her mother's hat suddenly ripened into cherries.

'Oh!' Mrs Harris said. 'I'd no idea!'

'Even Tom Handley's looking better. Eat up your egg.'

'She loves that Tom Handley really, you know. Always has.'

For the first time, Ivan looked at the bride with some interest.

'Why is she marrying Marcus, then?'

'Tom never asked her.'

'Why didn't she ask Tom?'

'She's not that saucy!' Mrs Harris chuckled at the sheer shockingness of the idea.

'*Saucy?* Well, what would you call marrying poor old Marcus, just to spite Tom?'

Mrs Harris hedged on her favourite's behalf:

'Tom Handley's had his chances. It's his own fault. He brought this on himself. That Tom's so stubborn he'd walk right round the orchard twice and pick himself a crab apple at last.'

'That doesn't excuse Angela.'

'Sshh! Here comes Reverend Collins. You hush now.'

The vicar spread out his arms to the congregation. The joyous organ music filled out richly as the first credits rose. The camera swooped up to the rafters and hovered there, loftily, through the remaining credits, until the screen went blank. Sighing with pleasure, Mrs Harris leaned back, satisfied, in her armchair.

'He's looking better, Reverend Collins is. He looked quite ill, I thought, last Tuesday.'

'Green, was he?'

She didn't answer. She had her head down over her supper. Her hands flapped nervously around the sides of the tray, touching the plate here, shifting the cup around on its saucer, as if she kept forgetting what she was about.

'Eat up your egg.'

'I can't.' Fretfully, she pushed the tray away. Ivan shot his hands out to steady it before it fell onto the floor.

'What's up? What's wrong with it?'

'Where is Natasha? Natasha knows how I have my egg. Where's Natasha?'

'Natasha's out.'

'Well, Henry then. Fetch Henry.'

'Henry's out, too. They're both out. How *do* you have your egg?'

'Mind your own business! I don't want you to bring me my egg.'

'It is my business now. I'm going to be bringing you your egg quite often. I thought you liked them hard.'

She scrabbled on the tray for the egg spoon. Her stiff fingers chased it over the smooth surface until it slid from sight under the rim of the plate. Ivan fished it out for her, and put it in her hand.

'Shall I take off the top for you?'

Deftly, he sliced the egg's top off.

She laid the spoon down on the tray again and tried to push the tray at him. He pushed it back and tea slopped over the edge of her cup into the saucer.

'You've got to *eat*.'

'Don't tell me what to do!'

'What's *wrong* with it?'

'It isn't in a cup! That's how I have my eggs. I have them chopped up in a teacup, where I can get at them, with salt and butter. You ought to *know* that!' Her whole body trembled with vexation. Patches of colour widened on her cheeks and she breathed hard. She swatted out at the eggshell she was too old and unhandy to manage, and both of them watched as the eggcup toppled over and the egg rumbled in an unsteady heavy hard-boiled arc across the tray.

Ivan said:

'I didn't know.'

He looked down at her, suddenly seeing her, how old and little and feeble she had become. Sophie would have come out immediately with something reassuring like: 'How was I supposed to know you eat your eggs the same way I do, out of a teacup?' But he wasn't Sophie. He picked the tray up and walked out of the room.

He came back ten minutes later. This time the tray held three cups, one with her tea and two with eggs in them, fresh-boiled and chopped into bits with salt and dabs of butter. He'd even cut the buttered toast into short manageable strips.

Again, he dislodged the dozing cat to lay the tray down in her lap.

'Lovely,' she said.

He watched her pick a toast strip up and prod it firmly into the yellowy mess in the cup. He picked his own up and copied her. For all that it looked so peculiar, it tasted pretty good, he thought. Better than plain old boiled egg. He tucked in, quite enjoying it.

After a while, as she sipped tea, he asked companionably:

'Was that the right amount of salt for you?'

'Just the job,' Mrs Harris said. 'Hunky-dory! I wouldn't mind if you brought me my egg every day.'

'I may yet,' Ivan muttered.

She looked at him with curiosity.

'Bit of a turnabout in the kitchen? All change?'

Trapped, Ivan temporized.

'There was a bit of a fuss, yes. It was agreed that Henry and Natasha needed some more time to themselves – out of the house – so the rest of us have had to take over some of the jobs.'

'And you offered to bring in my eggs!'

He tried to simply leave it there; but it wasn't in him.

'Well . . . Not exactly. I mean, you see, we held a sort of toss-up for each job.'

'And you won.'

Ivan would, right that moment, have sold his soul for Sophie's kind and easy tongue.

'No, actually. I lost.'

Her face burned with hurt. Wanting the fat warm comforting cat in her lap, not the old tray, she shoved the wooden hardness of it away from her. Ivan caught hold of it just in time, and swung it away, out of danger.

'I'll get the timing better tomorrow,' he promised. 'I'll get the supper all over with before the programme starts, so we won't miss any.'

It was the best that he could do. And, upset as she was, she did not miss this quiet offer of his to sit with her and keep her company. After a moment she looked up and told him bravely and politely:

'I'll hand it to you, for a loser you've been very gracious. You certainly do know how to carry the dead cockerel home from the fight.'

Ivan said, equally politely:
'And so do you.'

All change

Tanya trailed into Mrs Harris's room with the hot water-bottle and nearly dropped it in astonishment.

'Gran!' Tanya said. 'You're all changed round!'

She looked up at where Ivan stood in his socks on the dresser sticking up on the wall a poster of a woman lying, star-fish fashion, alone, on wide and glaring desert sand. The sun above her bleached all the colour from the huge sky, it burned so fiercely. The peaks of the far mountains were tinged red-hot.

'Ivan, that girl has got no clothes on.'

'The prettiest birthday suit I ever saw,' said Mrs Harris. 'Look at her, toasting on both sides. That girl knows how many beans in a bag make five.'

Tanya looked round. The bed was somewhere new. So was the chest of drawers. The television, too.

'You've moved the television,' Tanya accused her brother.

'Reception's better there,' Ivan said. 'That's how all this got started. If I have to sit through *Fairways* and *Solomon Street* every evening, I'll make sure that the picture's clear.'

'He knows his onions with that telly,' Mrs Harris said proudly. 'He's got the colour perfect. I can't tell you how much better the Reverend Collins is looking.'

'Where's all Gran's china things, off the dresser?'

'In that box under there.'

'Why have you put them there?'

'They gather dust,' said Ivan. 'I've got no time for dusting. Out they go.'

'Can I have some of them?'

'Yes,' Mrs Harris said. 'You can have some of them now and all of the rest as soon as I'm dead. The last gown I'll be modelling won't have any pockets.'

Tanya looked round to see what else she fancied. Along the wall, above the bed, there was another poster that had not been there the last time she came in. This one was amazingly wide, a strip of huge incoming sea, great green voluptuous rolling caverns of foaming waves and crashing surf and spinning spume. It was so green and wide and huge and strong, it sucked you in when you began to look at it.

'Gosh!' Tanya breathed. 'Where did that come from?'

'Print-It!' said Ivan. 'Smashing, isn't it?'

'It makes me dizzy, looking,' Mrs Harris told her. 'I keep on seeing pirates behind the dresser.' She added, a little wistfully: 'I should have spent my life beside the sea.'

Ivan jumped down. He lifted two more framed pictures off their wall hooks.

'I didn't like the lady on the left,' Mrs Harris remarked. 'She was pernickety. I won't miss her. But I shall miss that stag on the hillside. I like that stag. I understand him and he understands me.'

Ivan dumped the picture of the lady in the box, and laid the picture of the stag on the table.

'I'll put him back up somewhere else once I've got this last poster up.'

'What's this one, then?'

'You'll like this,' Ivan said. He unrolled the third, enormous poster. 'It came out very well, considering.'

He held as much of it as he could hold up for her to see, and grinned at her as she peered at it short-sightedly.

'Gosh!' Tanya said. 'Ivan!'

A very old woman sat in a back garden on a wooden chair, holding an enormous cat asleep on her lap. She peered a little short-sightedly towards the camera. Someone had stuck a daisy in her hair.

Mrs Harris chuckled with pleasure.

'Ivan, that cat is just the spit and image of Lucy here.'

'Of course it is. It *is* Lucy, isn't it?'

'Lucy? My Lucy? On that big poster? Never!'

'Lucy and you. Last summer, in the garden. Dad took a lot of photos. Don't you remember?'

'Me? Me and Lucy?' She peered even harder at the poster. 'Ivan! That's my chair! Those are Natasha's naughties on that washing line! Oh, Ivan, it *must* be me and Lucy.' She stared at it. 'But it's so big!'

'It's blown up, isn't it? I got it blown up into a poster.'

'The things you see if you live long enough!'

She stared and stared.

'That's me and Lucy? Really?'

'Really.'

'It is, too.' She stroked the cat fast and hard, hoping to wake her. 'Lucy. Look at us. Don't we look nobs? Don't we look just the thing? We wouldn't see a soul in the park who we'd like better than ourselves, would we, Lucy? No, we would not!'

'Are you done? Can I put it on the wall now?'

'Oh, well I never. Me and my Lucy. Go on, then. Don't just stand there like a dumb cluck. Hang it up on the wall. Be careful now. Mind you don't rip us, me and Lucy. You watch what you're about.'

When Ivan and Tanya left, she was still admiring herself and her cat. Back in the kitchen Tanya said:

'You'll catch it when they get to see what you've done.'

Ivan said:

'It's Gran's room. It's Gran's business.'

He thought she'd argue. But she just shrugged and said:

'I expect you're right. Now that they only have to pop in every now and then to see that she's all right, they're much more easy-going about everything.'

'They can afford to be,' said Ivan, with feeling.

Homework

Ivan strode into Mrs Harris's room, whistling. He swung the sherry bottle temptingly from his fingers.

'Telly off, Gran,' he said, flicking the switch. 'It's homework time again.'

She woke with a start that set her wispy white hair trembling.

'Oh, it's you, dear. I was just nodding off.'

'Just nodding off! You've been unconscious ever since *The Glumps.*'

'I have not. I was resting my eyes.'

'Rubbish!'

She watched him fondly and admiringly as he set things up just as usual. He hooked his little stool closer to her chair with his foot, and poured a large amount of sherry into yesterday's sticky glass. He fetched a pen from her dresser and pulled a bright red notebook out from where he kept it, under her armchair. He sat down beside her, rooting through the notebook, still whistling softly under his breath.

'We won't miss *Fairways* on the telly, will we?'

'No,' Ivan said. 'It's *Solomon Street* today.'

'I thought that was tomorrow, dear.'

'It was, yesterday.'

'What about *Fairways*? I thought that was today.'

'It will be, tomorrow.'

Confused, she surrendered.

'You won't let me miss any of whichever it is, will you, dear?'

'Come on, Gran. You know the rules. You can't watch telly till you've done my homework.'

Mrs Harris beamed at him.

'Yes, dear. Where were we, dear?'

Ivan flicked through his notes.

'This business of eating a dead mouse to cure the whooping cough,' he said. 'Were you just raving? Did I give you too much sherry?'

'Oh, no, dear. My mother swore that that was very, very common. The mothers used to send to the town for the doctor, she said. "He'll have to come," they'd say. "He'll have to come. She's had her mouse, and still she's no better."'

'Disgusting. And cobwebs to bind cuts? Did you mean that?'

'Works a fair treat. You ought to try it.'

'And ivy leaves soaked in vinegar for corns?'

'That's right, dear.'

'And warm onions in the ear, for ear ache?'

'Not onions, dear. You can't have been listening properly. Shallots. A small piece of shallot in nice warm oil.'

'What about coughs? Did we get to coughs?'

'Coughs? Oh, the coughing. The coughing.' Her voice softened suddenly. Even the wrinkles on her face seemed to flatten a little as she thought back, way back. 'The coughing in that school. Oh, dear, oh, dear, I'd clean forgotten. It went on all day, on and on, on and on. You could hardly hear poor old Miss Davenport at times, for all the coughing. The *noise* of it. Like barking, it was. As bad as that. It never stopped the whole winter. It was cough-cough, cough-cough, all through, and right into spring. The fire could hardly lift the chill, you see. Some days it got so cold in there, the ink froze in our pots. Some years we weren't all better again till you could step on six daisies at once.'

Ivan wrote in his notebook:

No antibiotics. Endless coughing, probably low-grade pneumonia. Summer – step on six daisies at once.

He said:

'Did these cures work? This chilblain cure, for example. Did that work?'

'I don't believe it can have, really, dear. We were all covered in them, hands and feet. You couldn't cram your toes into your boots, half the time, without crying. We even had chilblains on our knees and our ears.'

'It sounds quite horrible.'

'And people didn't even think about it. That's how it goes.'

'It doesn't go that way with me. I'd think about it.'

'Oh, you. You're your father's child. You'll be a union man for sure.'

'Henry? A union man?'

'Alfred.'

'My *grand*father.'

'Yes, dear.'

He saw it made no difference to her, and so he left it.

'That's why he came to London, the union

work. I didn't mind. I believed in it, too. More than him, in the end, I came to think. He only saw what still lay there to be done. I saw the changes behind us. You don't see chilblains on the children's knees any more. You don't see children's knees at all from November to April. But making things better is sad, slow work.'

'You weren't hard-boiled revolutionaries.'

'We were soft souls. We could have done without the battle at all.' Her hands plucked at the ends of her woollen cardigan and, momentarily, her voice drifted away. 'I think back now to all the time it took up, time when we could have been simply living our lives, just being together like two companionable cows in a field, and I sometimes wonder if I would do it all over again.'

Ivan said sternly:

'You'd have to. You'd have to simply because it would be there, still waiting to be done.'

'Maybe. I suppose so.' She added, stubbornly, after a little pause: 'But, still, I wouldn't have minded being born a cow in a meadow with all that time to myself. Time to stand quietly and watch the grass grow. Time to keep still so all the birds came near.' She chuckled quietly to herself. 'I'm making up for it now, though. I'm like a cow, now that I'm old.' She nodded up at the poster of herself and Lucy, on the wall. 'Look at us. Some days we settle down on that old chair and watch Natasha running about, pegging sheets on that washing line, and we sit quiet the livelong day, just like we are up there, and watch them drying.'

'Watch them drying? All *day*?'

'And listen.'

'Listen?'

'Listen.' The freckled old hands flapped in the air, trying to show him. 'Flap-flap, flap-flap. That's how it goes. We sit against the side of the house for long enough, and after a while we get to feeling a part of it, me and Lucy. The house bakes in the sunshine and so do we. I like the summer best now. Your father always preferred the spring—'

'My *grand*father.'

'Yes, dear.' She didn't even hear him. 'And spring is nice. But summer's better . . .'

Her voice trailed off again. After a moment, Ivan stood up and turned the television on.

'Back to earth, Gran,' he told her. 'Telly time.'

Pigs

'What about pigs?'

'Pigs?'

'Did you keep pigs?'

'Pigs?' She looked confused. 'Pigs? Yes.' The old face struggled with a memory. 'My mother's mother—'

'My great *great* grandmother.'

'She told my mother once that when she was young and times were very hard, and they ran out of acorns all about, her father boiled up her cat's drowned kittens to feed the pig.'

They sat in silence. Ivan thought back to the elaborate funeral that Tanya and Nicholas gave their dead terrapin. He didn't know what she was thinking, and didn't like to ask.

Rock cakes

Overtaking Ivan on the walk home from school, Sophie swung her book bag happily into her brother's back.

'Careful,' he warned. 'Don't jog.'

'What's in that box you're carrying?'

'Rock cakes. Miss Higgins said that they were excellent.'

'Rockier than anyone else's, were they?'

'Would you like to try one?'

'No, thanks. I can't afford to get weighed down tonight. I'm going back to school to help paint the backcloth for the school play.'

'You? You've been chosen to help paint the backcloth?'

'Yes. Me. Picasso Harris,' Sophie said proudly.

She pushed the garden gate open for Ivan and his box of rock cakes. Halfway up the path, they caught up with Tanya and Nicholas. Over his jacket Nicholas was wearing a huge scarlet apron. Tanya crouched behind him, bent over, trying to undo the knot in the apron strings with her teeth.

'What's that extraordinary thing you're wearing?' Ivan asked Nicholas.

'My apron,' Nicholas said. 'It's finished. It's taken me eight weeks to make and now Tanya's pulled the bow into a knot and I'll be stuck in it for ever.'

'I only tugged at one of the ends,' Tanya

defended herself. 'If you'd learn to tie bows like other people tie bows, it simply would have come undone when I pulled it.'

'Doesn't Nicholas know how to tie bows?'

'Why should I know how to tie bows?' Nicholas's face reddened. 'I'm not a *girl*.'

Sophie and Ivan stood by and waited while Tanya unpicked the tangle. Then the four of them rushed into the house in a bunch and made for the kitchen, where Natasha was standing, leaning against the cupboard door, dressed to go out, tapping her foot with impatience.

'You're all very late,' she told them. 'I have been waiting.'

Ivan placed the box of cakes upon the table in front of her with a triumphant flourish.

'Look!' he said. 'Rock cakes. I made them. They're very good indeed. Have one.'

'I *deserve* one,' said Tanya, dipping in and choosing the largest. 'I wrote an essay today, three pages long, and Mr Belvoir stuck it up on the wall. He said it was to serve as an inspiration to those in the class who had hardly started.'

'My apron's finished,' Nicholas declared, turning around like a model. 'What do you think of it? My hemming was so neat, I was allowed to use the sewing machine to finish the band.'

'Is there anything to eat?' Sophie asked, looking around the kitchen. 'I'm starving, but I can't stay in for supper. I have to go back to school to help paint trees on the backcloth for the school play. Only four were chosen, and I was one.'

Natasha snatched up her coat from where it lay over the back of a chair.

'Very nice,' she said, indicating the box of rock cakes. 'Very good,' she said, nodding at the new apron. 'I'm very pleased about the essay,' she told Tanya. 'I hope you have a very nice time,' she told Sophie. 'But now you've come back at last, I must be off at once. I'm very late.'

She gave each one of them in turn a hasty peck on the cheek, and then made for the door.

'There's bacon pie in the oven,' she said. 'Your father and I won't be back for supper. I'm meeting him at the dance hall for an early class, and then we're going out for dinner. Don't forget to rinse the salad properly, and remember Granny can't manage pie crust unless it's cut up first. Take care. Goodbye.'

The kitchen door shut behind her. The children listened to the light tap-tap-tapping of her high heels along the hall, past Granny's room.

The front door banged, and there was silence.

None of the children moved. Nobody spoke.

After a few moments Nicholas began to struggle, red-faced, out of his apron. Once free of its folds, he pounded the bright material into a bunch and threw it angrily on to the table.

'"Very nice"', he repeated, sarcastically, under his breath in the faint accent they all associated with Natasha. "Very good. I'm very pleased. Have a very nice time. But I'm afraid I'm very late. Your supper's in the oven. Goodbye."

'Come off it,' Sophie said. 'It's not that bad.'

'It *is*!' shrieked Nicholas. 'It *is* that bad!'

He looked around him wildly. Then suddenly he reached into Ivan's box on the table and snatching up a handful of rock cakes, he flung them, fiercely, at the door through which Natasha had just left. The rock cakes shattered into tiny fragments that fell all over the floor.

The others watched him in silent concern. Then Sophie said:

'Good rock cakes, Ivan. You've got some first-rate ammunition there for your next family revolution.'

Tanya said sourly:

'I'm not clearing that mess up, Nicholas. Not

even if I'm down on Ivan's schedule for sweeping the floor.'

'Pass the brush,' Ivan said. 'I'll sweep it up. All this is my fault, after all.'

Sad, slow work

'What did you mean when you said what you did about making things better?'

'What did I say, dear?'

'You said that it was sad, slow work.'

'Did I say that?'

'Yes. Yes, you did. And I've been thinking about it. I thought at first maybe you meant that things went slowly because you planned it that way. You weren't prepared to take the risk of making changes too quickly, in case they went wrong and things got worse instead of better, and you were sad about that. Then I thought maybe you truly believed that only the small changes – like no more chilblains on the children's feet – really count; and all the big things people become real bomb-throwing revolutionaries about don't, in the end, add up to much to most people. That's what Sophie thinks. She says that revolution's for the birds. She says only things like family planning and inoculations and hostels for the homeless really matter. She says if you can't look back at the end of any one day and point to someone better off for what you did in those eight hours, you might as well forget it.'

'Mustn't forget it.'

'What?'

'*Solomon Street.*'

Ivan ignored her.

'Sophie says revolutionary ideals, like ridding the world of capitalism or something, are just high-blown rubbish and any sensible person would trade them in for a child health clinic any day.'

'Is it time yet, dear?'

'Time? What for? Oh, for *Solomon Street*. Not yet, no. Plenty of time. Tanya thinks Sophie's absolutely wrong. She says, "You offer one or two more child health clinics and a bit more food to people who want something that really matters to them, like their country's freedom or a proper vote, and they'll spit in your eye and say: 'No, thanks. We'll take the freedom and a proper vote, then we'll be free to vote to build our own child health clinics, and lots more besides."' She's right there, too.'

'It must be nearly seven, dear.'

'Nicholas said maybe I didn't understand you right, and what you meant was it was either one thing or the other. Sad work if it goes big and fast, with guns and blood and damage; slow if it's just the plod, plod, plod of one law here, one citizens' advice bureau there. But that can't be right. Revolutions aren't sad. They'd never so much as get off the ground if they were sad. Look at the posters of the leaders. They don't look sad.'

'It must be time to switch on now, dear.'

'I don't get it at all. I asked Natasha what she thought of revolutionaries. She's Russian, after all. You'd think she of all people would have a sensible opinion. Do you know what she said?'

'No, dear.'

'I'm not sure, either. Something bleak and Russian. Dad says it sounds like: "They pray so hard for good weather that drought sets in." What use is that?'

'It must be time, dear. Just so the set has time to warm up.'

'Sets don't warm up now, Gran. That was before the war, when sets warmed up.'

Maybe the clock's a little bit slow, though.'

'Clocks aren't slow any more, either. That was before the war, too, when clocks went slow. You really ought to try and keep up. I asked Dad, too, you know. It's unbelievable, what he said when I asked him. Do you know what he said?'

'No, dear.'

'He said: "Don't ask me, son." Can you believe that? What use is that? I don't know what to think, I really don't.'

'Let's put the notebook away now, dear. You must have got enough down by now.'

'This isn't for the project, Gran! I was just thinking about it. This is for *me*!'

Don't say it, Tanya

Back in the kitchen, Tanya was grumbling:
'Where's Ivan, anyway? Why hasn't he started on supper yet?'

'He's in with Granny, watching *Solomon Street*.'

'According to this schedule he's put up on the fridge, either Sophie can't go to orchestra tomorrow night, or one of us will have to give up swimming.'

'I'm not giving up another thing this week,' Sophie said. 'I've already done far more than my fair share.'

'We've all done more than our fair share.'

'If I have to take her one more cup of milky coffee, I shall spit in it first.'

'These sheets *stink*,' Nicholas complained. 'This is the fourth load I've done since Monday.' He slammed the machine door shut irritably. 'We're almost out of washing powder, too. Why hasn't Ivan got another box?'

'He didn't get down to Cost-Cut in time. Mum was late back and he couldn't leave Granny.'

'He should have picked it up yesterday.'

'They went out yesterday as well.'

'He'd better not forget tomorrow.'

'They're going out again tomorrow.'

'Well, why can't he go now?'

'Because they're still out.'

'We're still here, aren't we? Why can't he just run down and get it now?'

'Nicholas, it's not just washing powder, you

know. We're out of tons of stuff. The coffee jar's almost empty. We're all out of those tins of rice pudding she eats. She's still waiting for her peppermints. We haven't got this week's *Radio Times* yet. If he goes off to get them now he'll be at least an hour, so one of us will have to miss swimming.'

'I'm not missing swimming.'

'I was late last week. That was Ivan's fault, he took so long down at Cost-Cut.'

'Maybe they'll get home before it closes, and Ivan can go then.'

'They won't be back for hours. They're out dancing.'

'Dancing!'

'Again? That's the third time since Saturday!'

'He's working on his turns.'

'It's better than woodwork evening,' Tanya said. 'I can't *stand* woodwork evening. "Where is my chisel? Where'd you put my clamp? Has anybody seen my fretsaw? Who's touched my dowelling rods?" I can't stand woodwork evening, I tell you.'

'It's better than her Italian night. The next time she sails in at ten o'clock and says "*Molto bene*" to my ironing pile, I'm going to strangle her with one of her own pairs of tights.'

'I've still got *piles* of homework to do.'

'I'm going up to do mine right now. If this machine packs up on rinse again, Ivan will have to hang around to reset it.'

'Well, he can put these dishes away while he's at it. We'll all be late for swimming if we're not careful.'

'Is Ivan coming?'

'If they get back in time he will.'

'They won't though, will they? Not if it's dancing.'

'No. No, they won't.'

'Poor Ivan,' Sophie said. 'If he misses swimming again tonight, then that will be for the third time in a row and he'll be dropped from the team for certain.'

Tanya and Nicholas glanced at one another uncomfortably. Then Tanya said:

'There's nothing we can do about that.'

Nicholas said nothing.

'We could do more to help him,' Sophie suggested. 'After all, it's mostly only sitting with Granny and bringing her trays of food and little things like that. Mum still does most of the housework. Dad still buys most of the food. It's really only little things . . .'

'Those little things are *endless*,' said Tanya. 'Last week I went in there with salt for her breakfast egg, and by the time I'd done all the "little things" she wanted – opened the curtains, switched on the fire, found her reading glasses, told her what day it was – and then escaped again, there wasn't even time for me to do my packed lunch. It's worse for Nicholas. He doesn't even have the nerve to walk out while she's still talking to him, like I do.' She turned to her brother and told him fiercely: 'Tell Sophie what happened yesterday. Go on!'

Nicholas looked down at the floor and said nothing.

'I'll tell her, then,' cried Tanya. 'His friends went off without him and he cried.' Nicholas began to shake his head, but Tanya persisted: 'Oh, yes. I saw you. You were crying.'

'What happened?' Sophie asked him.

Tanya said scornfully, before he could answer:

'Oh, just one of those "little things". Ivan asked Nicholas to take Granny's tea in. Nicholas's friends were waiting for him on the doorstep but Ivan promised him that it would only take a moment. Nicholas was trapped in there for twenty-five minutes. It was that long before he escaped. His friends had all gone off by then, of course. Fed up with waiting.'

'Oh, dear,' said Sophie.

'*See?*' Tanya cried. 'One little thing after another. You take her in a plate of biscuits and then it's pillow-plumping and water-fetching and TV channel-changing and answering silly questions about what you did today at school. We just can't stand it. That's why we only go in there when Ivan makes us.'

'I didn't realize,' Sophie said.

'Of course you didn't. You're never here. You whip through whatever little job Ivan wrote down for you on the schedule, and then you rush up to your room and hide among your homework books until it's quite safe to come down again.'

'I come down just as soon as I've finished!'

'You could have fooled us,' Tanya retorted. 'You always seem to come down just as soon as Ivan has finished settling Granny down for the night!'

Sophie's face reddened with guilt and temper, both fuelled by her sister's brutal frankness. She hit back:

'You two don't help either. You've admitted it.'

'No. We don't help. And we don't really care if

you don't either. It's Ivan's problem and it's Ivan's fault. All this is his fault. He got himself into this, and he can stew in it as long as he likes. All that he has to do to stop it is to tell them that he doesn't care any more if—'

Sophie sprang at her.

'Don't say it, Tanya!' she shouted. 'Don't say it!'

'I don't think I
want rescuing . . .'

Another Granny project

Sophie came into Ivan's room so fast he had no time to hide the bright red notebook he was writing in. As soon as Sophie saw her brother trying to look casual, she swooped. She snatched the notebook out of his hands.

'What's this, then?'

She turned it over. Written on the front was:

The Granny Project, by Ivan Harris. For Social Science

'Oh, not again! You must be *mad*.'

'I don't see why. I have to do another project. She's sitting there. I'm sitting with her. It's tit for tat. I boil her eggs, she does my homework. Some of it's very interesting.'

Sophie let all the pages flick past, then

something he'd written caught her eye. She stuck her finger down to trap the page.

'Yuk!' she said. 'Eeeyuk!'

'Is that the bit about them eating mice?'

'God, no. It's worse than that. It's the bit when you say they blew their noses with their fingers.'

'Sophie, you've seen people doing that in swimming pools.'

She gazed at him in horror, absolute horror.

'No! Ivan! It's not true! Not Bonnington Pool!'

'You must have seen. It happens all the time.'

'I can't see *anything* without my lenses. I can hardly see where the water starts. Oh, tell me it's not true!'

'It's not true.'

'It is, though, isn't it?'

'It happens all the time.'

'Yeeuk! *Disgusting!* I'll *never* swim again.' She meant it.

'Would you take over Granny on Friday, then, so I can go? I haven't been for weeks.'

'That's what I came to talk to you about. I have a plan – a plan to rescue you.'

He turned away, not realizing that she could see him just as clearly as before, in the mirror.

'I don't think I want rescuing,' he said. 'Well,

not yet, anyway. Certainly not until the project's over and done with.'

'Then will you?'

'I don't know. Probably. Yes. I'm not sure.'

She watched him curiously. When he looked up again, he saw her watching him in the mirror. He blushed.

'I'll let you know,' he said.

'Just give the word,' she said, 'the moment you're ready. The plan is here' – she tapped her head – 'on the back burner, ready and waiting.'

'That's very good of you.'

'It's nothing.'

To cover his embarrassment, she turned her attention back to the notebook in her hand. She ran a few more pages between her fingers.

'Her grandparents didn't really separate the cockerel from the hens every Sunday?'

'That's nothing.' He bounded up to her side. 'Here, look. Did you know this. Did you know Granny was sent up to bed without any supper for standing watching some cow calve?'

'She never told me that. Where is it?'

'It's just a few pages further on, in the next section, the one on *Religion and Sunday*, after *Sickness and Health*.'

'Thorough as usual.' She flicked further on, and what she saw on the way convulsed her with laughter. She dropped on her brother's bed.

'Which bit? Which bit, Sophie?'

She couldn't say. She couldn't catch her breath for long enough to explain. He leaned across her to see what she was laughing at, but she hugged the notebook to herself as she fell about on the bed. He pummelled her and pummelled her, but she couldn't tell him, she was laughing so hard. He prised the notebook out from between her fingers and held the double page she'd stopped at up in front of her face. She pulled herself together just long enough to stab at the paragraph with her finger.

'Oh, that! *Handbag!* Is that all?'

Handbag

'Handbag?'

'Yes. Handbag.'

'That's what they called it?'

'Yes. Sophie told me. She read it in Ivan's new Granny Project.'

'I don't believe it. *Handbag.*'

Tanya said:

'I think it's rather sweet and suitable.'

'Suitable?' Nicholas was baffled.

'Yes. That's what it would look like, in a way.'

'A pretty funny way, if you ask me.'

'Well, yes. But still, you can see why they called it that.'

'I can't. I can't see it at all.'

'Not at all?'

'No.'

'You should try drawing it. See what it looks like then.'

'That's silly.'

Tanya went out to fetch some moss for her Japanese Garden Project. While she was gone, Nicholas took out a pencil and a pad of paper. On the first clean sheet he drew a bull. It was, when he had finished it, so very unlike a bull that he ripped the sheet of paper out of the pad and bunched it up and threw it in the basket beside him. He tried again. His second bull was better. So slowly, with enormous care, between the bull's hind legs Nicholas drew testicles and a penis. He stared at them for quite some time, then rubbed them out.

When Tanya came back in, he told her:
'They wouldn't look like a handbag at *all*.'

Baked feathers

Natasha swung the oven door back and clouds of feathers flew up in her face.

'Blast!'

She slammed the door closed, making matters worse. The feathers swirled about her in hundreds, like lazy locusts, black and white and grey and blown, and even brilliant green and blue and turquoise. They floated down her neck and caught in her hair. They settled on her thin shoulders.

'Hell! Blast!'

'What is it?' Henry asked, coming in. 'What's going on? Natasha, what are you doing with all these feathers?'

'I?' Natasha ground her teeth. 'I? It is not I who filled the stove with filthy fetid feathers!'

Nicholas leaped about with the plastic colander, trying to catch as many feathers as he could before they touched the kitchen floor, and failing to catch any.

'They're not filthy and fetid,' he said. 'They're nice and clean. Cleaner than anything else around here. And if you hadn't opened up the door, they'd have been sterilized in just twenty minutes.'

Natasha leaned across the kitchen table and, seizing him by the shirt collar, she hissed:

'What are you up to, little one?'

'Let go of him. You don't know that it's him.'

'В тихом омути волятся.'

Nicholas tore himself free, terrified. He ran behind his father, who said:

'She didn't threaten to kill you, you know. She only said that devils live in quiet ponds.'

'I'm *not* a quiet pond.'

'Tsssk! Feather-cooker!'

Henry said:

'Be more methodical, Natasha. Start at the start. Ask him whose feathers he was cooking.'

'Whose feathers, little feather-cooker? Whose feathers were you cooking? I ask you.'

'Nobody's in particular.'

She flew at him. Hastily he said:

'Some of them were from my collection. A lot

159

of them were Granny's hat. Sophie had one or two. Ivan found a few. Tanya remembered where she'd seen a dead blackbird—'

'Dead blackbird feathers! *Carrion?* In my *stove*?'

'It isn't really just *your* stove, you know. You hardly use it any more. You only eat cheese sandwiches these days. If it were anybody's stove, it would be Ivan's now.'

'He steals my stove?'

'He uses it.'

'For cooking feathers!'

'Not only feathers. He cooks hundreds of things. Eggs, cheese on toast, baked beans and sausages. He made us curried beef last night.'

'Do not try to distract me from feathers!'

'All right,' Nicholas surrendered fairly graciously. 'Feathers it is.'

Henry said:

'Nicholas, would you mind simply explaining to Natasha here exactly what is going on, apropos feathers.'

'You shake him! He will answer faster!'

'Natasha!'

'Tsssk!'

'We're making Granny a new pillow.'

Natasha's lip curled into a thin knot.

'To lay her head on? Or to eat?'

Nicholas answered with dignity:

'To rest against.'

'Your grandmother asked you for a pillow?'

'No. It was Tanya's idea. She thought Granny might like a special pillow for her birthday. The reason why it's so special is that we're making it the old-fashioned way.'

Natasha indicated feathers caught in the plant leaves, stuck on the butter, floating a finger deep in the cat's bowl of water.

'This is the old-fashioned way?'

'It's the way she told Ivan about, for his project.'

'Another project!' she screamed, and beat the airing cupboard door with her fists. 'I will blow that school up from its foundations to the weathervane. Since we have no plagues, we must suffer projects!'

'And, the old-fashioned way, before you put the feathers in the pillow, you bake them in the oven to kill all the insects.'

'Insects there are in this house that will not fit in that small oven!'

'There's no need to be rude. I doubt if you two

even thought to get poor Granny a present at all.'

Natasha scowled.

'A better present might have been to leave her favourite hat alone.'

Nicholas said:

'She didn't want it any more. She said so. She said she'd like to think of the blue feathers being there, under her head, at night. She said she didn't see the point of keeping the hat as a hat any longer. She said she didn't really believe that she'll be going outside much any more!'

He slammed out of the room, leaving them looking guiltily at one another through the great cloud of feathers his precipitous departure had stirred up once more.

Coming down with a cold

The words blurred into fuzz time and again as Ivan wrote them in the bright red notebook. He had some difficulty holding the pen until he realized that it was his hand that was shaking. Knowing the problem seemed to help a bit. He had to ask her to repeat it twice, but finally he got it down:

> *Four seeds you have to sow,*
> *One for rook and one for crow,*
> *One to die and one to grow.*

He blew his reddened nose again. The noise and juddering of the blow exploded fireworks in his sore brain.

'That is some cold, young man,' Mrs Harris scolded. 'You ought to be in bed, you look so peaky.'

'I'll be all right. Get on about the gleaners. I'm still confused. Why did the farmer shake the ones he distrusted?'

'So all the grain they'd hidden would fall out of their clothes. The same reason that he would make some thresher empty his boots before he left the threshing floor. My father told me every single grain belonged to the farmer until the policeman was gone.'

'What?' Ivan blew his nose again. 'Policeman? I thought you told me there was only one, for miles around. He couldn't possibly have watched every field.'

'Not real policeman. Policeman sheaf!'

Policeman sheaf

Ivan wrote, his head spinning from the nose-blow. Then he looked once again at what he'd written, and said:

'Policeman *sheaf*? What are you on about?' He blew his nose again. 'I can't make head or tail of anything you've told me tonight.'

'You ought to be in bed, you ought.'

'I'll stay till someone else gets back.'

'You ought to have a nice hot toddy. You ought to be tucked up, looked after.'

'I'll be all right.' Forgetting where they'd got to, he looked down at the last blur on the page and forced it, momentarily, into:

Policeman sheaf

It meant nothing to him. And this time, when he tried blowing his nose, his eyes began to stream. He wiped his nose gently instead and told her:

'Start again. Right from the beginning.'

'After the harvesting, my father told me, the gleaners would move through, and all they gleaned belonged to the farmer. He left one sheaf in every field – the policeman sheaf – to show what lay there still belonged to him. It was on guard, see? And everybody knew what it meant, and knew that everyone knew that they knew it. So, if the farmer suspected that you'd been out to get what wasn't yours yet, he'd shake you, hard, to see what fell from you, the same way he'd make his people on the threshing floor empty their boots in case they'd stuffed them full of his grain to feed their own chickens. After the policeman sheaf was taken out, the rule was finders-keepers again.'

'And was there very much to find by then?'

'I don't know. I wasn't there, was I? I'm not that old. These are just stories that I'm telling you. Things that I heard. I wasn't there.'

'When *was* all this, then?'

She didn't answer him, so Ivan said: 'Oh, never mind. I'll work it out.'

He shook his head, trying to clear the fog inside, and it hurt horribly. When it had settled down, stopped swirling, he tried again. 'You're eighty-seven now, right?'

'If you say so, dear.'

'So you were born in—' He tried to work it out. He tried to set the sum up in his head, a simple enough sum, he knew, but it eluded him, the way to put it, where to set numbers, which went which side of which and what to do with them, whether to add or take away or borrow . . .

She saw his face go ashen. Suddenly anxious, she put her hand out to stroke his dark fringe away from his swollen fiery eyes.

'I'd pack you off to bed, if you were mine.'

'I am yours,' Ivan said, and saying it he slid, unconscious, from the little stool onto the floor at her feet.

A hostage to fortune

Natasha, coming home later to the news of Ivan's collapse, dropped her coat where she stood, in the hallway, and gripped her daughter by the arms.

'What did the doctor say? You tell me, quick.'

Sophie said, grinning:

'He said that his initial ausculatory examination—'

'In translation, Sophie! At once!'

Sophie's face dropped. She said in a sullen

monotone: 'He said Ivan had a filthy rotten cold and needed several days in bed unless it was to turn into worse.'

'Thank God!'

Natasha let go, and sank down weakly on the bottom stair.

Sophie rubbed blood back into the sudden patches on her arms and asked her mother, a little sourly:

'What on earth did you *think* it was?'

'Who can tell what I thought? Children are hostages to Fortune from the first.'

'Ivan is not a child. He's—'

'What do you know about it? Is he yours? Where is he?'

'He's fast asleep in bed.'

'Good. Good. I will go up and see him.'

'But Dad's already sitting with him. And he's asleep.'

'I'll see him sleeping for myself.'

She ran up the stairs and out of sight. Sophie picked up her mother's coat and, dusting off the fluff it had picked up in its fall, put it away on a hanger inside the cupboard. She strolled back thoughtfully into the kitchen, where Nicholas and Tanya huddled together making a matchstick pagoda for Tanya's Japanese garden project.

'She almost had a fit when I told her,' she said to them. 'It was amazing. She went as white as a sheet.'

Tanya said:

'Ivan's her favourite, isn't he? He always has been. I've always sort of known he was her favourite, but it's at times like this she proves it. He only fainted, after all. That's all he did.'

'Parents don't have favourite children,' Nicholas assured her.

'Oh, Nicholas!' scoffed Tanya.

Sophie sat down and handed the trimmed matches to them, one by one, as each of them glued their way up opposite sides of the tiny curved pointed roof.

'Ivan told me, a while ago, to hold off on any plans to rescue him,' she told them, still thoughtful. 'But if he's going to lie about in bed, ill, that surely changes everything. If we don't act now, to protect ourselves, we'll end up doing all our jobs and Ivan's too, and looking after both of them as well.'

'So think of something. Quick.'

'I am. I am. It's coming.'

Sophie leaned over the pile of matches, passing

and thinking, thinking and passing. The other two forbore from quarrelling, or even mentioning the flaws in one another's craftsmanship, they were so anxious not to break her train of thought. After a while, Sophie lifted her head and smiled at them.

'Got it,' she said.

'Goody!'

'Well done! How does it work? What do we do?'

'I've no time to explain. If it's to work, we have to do it straight away, tonight, while they're still feeling weak and guilty and relieved and grateful about Ivan not being properly ill. Listen, you clear all this pagoda stuff off the table right away, and start cooking supper. Search the kitchen for something. Look everywhere. See what's left in the fridge and what's in tins, and start on a meal. Make it as good and fancy as you can manage, and do a really good job of setting the table. Make it look a lot of work. Sweep up the bits off the floor. Find a clean tablecloth. Shine up those salt and pepper things, you know the sort of thing. Pretend it's guests. Get the best spread you can onto the table as soon as possible.'

'What about you?'

'I can't help you because I'm going upstairs. I

have some reading I have to get through, if this is to work.'

'What about them?'

'Don't let them in on it. Keep them out of here while you're getting everything ready, but make sure they're both in for supper. I think, after all this fuss, they won't be planning on going out this evening, but just make sure they don't.'

Tanya's eyes swept the drab messy kitchen and settled on the table, strewn with several days' clutter and leftover feathers.

'This had better work,' she warned her sister.

'It will, I promise. Now call me down just before the supper is ready to serve, and then, when they come in, fall in with everything I say. *Everything*, no matter how mad it sounds. Right?'

'Right!'

'Right!'

'Good old Sophie!'

'It's Sophie Superwoman again!'

A sacrificial lamb

Sophie pulled her head back away from the doorway.

'Quick,' she said. 'Here they come now.'

Nicholas picked up the glistening, steaming soup tureen and carried it across to the table. Tanya and Sophie stood at the ready behind their chair backs. The door flew open and in came Henry and Natasha, arm in arm, laughing.

'Good Lord,' said Henry, startled by the sudden dimness. 'Have we come into the wrong kitchen?'

Natasha didn't speak. She saw the silver glinting in the candlelight upon the wide fresh sweep of pure white linen cloth. Her eyes took in the low pile of fine china dinner plates beside the glowing soup tureen, the deftly folded napkins at each place, the sparkling cut-glass oil and vinegar bottles that she'd mislaid a couple of dinner parties ago, the bowl of flowers and, most of all, her son and daughters' steady expressionless faces.

'Tsssk!' she hissed softly under her breath. 'Something goes on.'

'Nonsense,' said Henry, hurt on the children's

behalf. 'Don't be so suspicious, Natasha. I think it's very good of them to lay all this lot on for us, after our fright.'

'Lay all what on?' asked Sophie.

'All this.' His arm swept round the room. 'All this arranging and tidying and setting and cooking. I think it's smashing of you all.'

'But we eat like this whenever you're both out,' Sophie said.

He laughed, and when she stared at him, her eyebrows lifted, and, taking their cue from her, Nicholas and Tanya raised their eyes at one another and shrugged, he said uneasily:

'What nonsense.'

'What?'

'That you eat this way whenever Natasha and I are out at night.'

'We do, though.' She turned to Nicholas and Tanya in turn. 'Don't we?'

'Yes.'

'Certainly.'

Henry took hold of Natasha's elbow and steered her to the place in front of the tureen. Just as he pulled her chair out for her, Sophie remarked:

'Actually, Nicholas usually sits there.'

'Since when?'

Henry's voice sounded a little bit sharp. Natasha, on the other hand, still didn't speak. She watched with quiet feline attentiveness.

'Since ages.' Sophie sought Nicholas's support again. 'Haven't you?'

'Oh, yes.'

'I see.'

Henry pulled out a different chair for Natasha. 'Is this all right?'

'That's fine.' Sophie sat down, snapping the web of tension that had begun to bind them all. 'Come on. Let's eat. I'm starving. Dish it up, Nicholas.'

His small pink tongue clenched fast between his teeth – serving the soup was tricky enough, serving as if you'd served it frequently for ages was something else again – Nicholas handed the first bowlful of soup across the table towards his mother. Henry intervened to take the dish from him, and said as he laid it down in front of Natasha:

'This smells delicious. I've not had this particular soup before.'

'We have this soup a lot,' said Sophie.

'All the time,' Tanya said, getting into the rhythm.

'I'm getting quite fed up with it myself,' said Nicholas.

'I suppose, yes, it is new to you two,' said Sophie.

'Who made it?'

Not certain if the answer had significance in Sophie's mysterious master plan, Tanya and Nicholas both looked non-committal.

'Tanya and Nicholas made it together tonight,' Sophie informed them firmly. 'But Ivan is the one who usually makes it. He generally serves it with croutons or garlic bread; but we've just had to manage how we could tonight, what with him not being around as usual to do it all.'

Astonished, Henry swirled the soup around in his bowl. He marvelled at the unusual consistency that Nicholas had achieved by adding, fast at the very end, two large dollops of soured cream straight from a tub he found in the fridge. He was impressed by the faint hint of tarragon that, unknown to him, Tanya had swiftly and cunningly infused from a spoonful of dried herbs in a teacup, and thrown in. He'd never, from the look and feel and taste of it, have guessed that four large tins of Heinz Cream of Tomato Soup lay, safely wrapped in newspaper, in the dustbin.

'Does Ivan cook like this often, then?'

'Oh, no! He usually takes much more time and care. It's just that sometimes, when he's exhausted from school and all the cleaning and shopping and looking after Granny, he has to let the cooking slide a bit. We don't mind, do we?'

'Oh, no.'

'Not at all.'

'In fact, we often tell him he ought to slacken off a bit more. We've seen this total physical collapse of his coming for weeks now, haven't we?'

'We warned him he was doing too much.'

'He never stops. Poor old Ivan.'

Henry was trying to break in, with a question, but Sophie said quickly:

'We *tell* him not to bother. We tell him that we'd far rather that he went upstairs for a rest, or try and get some of his homework done. We say we'd be happy to eat chips instead. But he *insists.*'

'Insists? Insists on cooking whenever Natasha and I are both out? Ivan?'

'He won't let us help, either. We offer all the time, but he keeps saying our homework and our swimming and music are far, far too important to miss. He won't let us share hardly any of the work, will he?'

'No.'

'Hardly any.'

'He says that it's important to him.'

'That's what he says.'

'Yes, that's what Ivan always says.'

'That it's the least that he can do for us, considering . . .'

'Considering *what*?'

Sophie didn't answer this. She broke the conversation off by briskly asking Tanya to pass along the empty soup bowls. In all the flurry of clearing the table, Henry glanced at Natasha several times, but she was watching her children piling the dishes on the draining board, reaching for oven cloths, politely making way for one another. She sat, still as an unsure animal, missing nothing.

Tanya brought over to the table a deep dish of glistening golden puff pastry triangles, and set them, sizzling deliciously, in front of Nicholas.

'Fantastic!' Henry said.

'A little disappointing,' said Sophie. 'But never mind.'

'Not quite as good as Ivan's, no,' Tanya said.

'Ivan's pastry is spectacular,' Nicholas said.

'Of course, he's had far more practice making it than any of us have.'

'He's got this knack of rolling it out right.'

'A very steady, experienced touch.'

Henry looked round at them. They all looked back at him perfectly steadily.

'So who made these tonight?'

Sophie stepped in before the other two could look at her for guidance again.

'We all did,' she told them. 'I made the spinach filling, and Nicholas made the pastry, and Tanya put it all together.'

'I'm not as neat as Ivan, though,' Tanya grumbled, poking disconsolately at her perfect machine-made triangles of fail-safe pastry from the packet that Nicholas had discovered at the very bottom of the freezer, and which he was now hoping he'd remembered to put in the dustbin along with the soup tins.

'There again,' Sophie consoled her. 'Ivan spends much more time than you do on these things. You have your homework every evening, after all.'

Natasha's eyes narrowed, and Henry, too, homed straight into the trap.

'Ivan has homework too, surely!'

Sophie waved a forkful of hot spinach in the air. 'Oh, *Ivan*! He's totally given up on homework these days. He has a shocking backlog – weeks and weeks. He says he's too discouraged even to try any longer. After all, he's always worked hard and done very well at school, before he got too tired and strained and frazzled to be able to concentrate on any of it any more. He used to be so capable. And now – to start failing after all these years of steady A grades—'

'Failing? Ivan? *Ivan?*'

She'd hoped he wouldn't push her for details on this. There was, after all, only one fail, and that was because of the Granny Project. But the schoolmaster in Henry rose to the top and rescued her. He panicked.

'*Fail?* I can hardly *believe* it. *Ivan?* Nobody has mentioned anything to me about this. Are you *sure?*'

'He doesn't *mind,*' said Sophie. 'Does he?'

'Oh, no.'

'He doesn't mind at all.'

'*I* mind,' said Henry. 'I mind a *lot.*'

'Well, Ivan doesn't. He puts us first, you see. He says that there's always a slim chance he may some day get another opportunity to educate himself, later in life. But there's only one chance we have to grow up in a safe and secure and nurturing family environment. He wouldn't want the rest of us to miss that, not for *anything*.' She spread her hands out over the table, brought home to them its safe and secure and nurturing order and warmth. 'Ivan says that a regular and comforting home background, with supporting rituals and systems, is doubly vital for the psychologically orphaned—'

'Psychologically *orphaned*?'

'That's right. He's thought about these things a good deal, Ivan has, and we've done work on it in Social Science. There are a lot of articles about the effects on growing children of familial depriv-ation and loss.'

'Familial deprivation and loss?'

'*And* separation and abandonment.'

'Separation? *Abandonment*?'

Sophie stared at him coolly over the table. 'It doesn't have to be *physical* abandonment, you know. The effects on the child of the psycho-logical withdrawal of parents can be almost as bad. Didn't either of you two ever do any Social Science? There's article after article on the topic by –' the names she'd read up on in the bedroom escaped her; she made up others – 'By Friedman and Winnipool and Chowley and Neave. You two go out a good deal nowadays. And at weekends, too. We see much less of you than we did before. Often you don't even eat with us. So Ivan's simply doing his best to compensate little Nicholas and Tanya here for your frequent absence.' Pretending to mistake his expression of shock and disbelief, she told him: 'It doesn't *matter* who fulfils the supportive parental role, or what their sex is. That's been proved time and time again by people like Hurley and McGrath and Rankin. Not R.P. Rankin – he's been discredited in the field. But Samuel Rankin, the American.' She challenged him with her eyes to refute the names she'd just made up on the spot to dumbfound him. 'It's all been known for years and *years*,' she said. 'It's taken for granted, all this early research, nowadays. Just like the stuff about family myths.'

'Family *myths*?'

'You know,' she told him. 'When some member of the family becomes subconsciously chosen to play a certain role in that family's myth. The Black Sheep or the Rising Star. The Sickly One, or, as in Ivan's case' – she stared him out – 'The Sacrificial Lamb!'

Henry looked horror-struck. The children waited. Natasha burst into tears.

Sophie rested her case.

Under the table, Tanya squeezed her sister's fingers, hard, to comfort her for telling all those lies.

A few days in bed

Ivan had never been so well looked after in his whole life. For four whole days he sat in state, propped up by all the pillows Natasha could find, sipping at jasmine tea and hot lemon toddies, nibbling chocolate biscuits, dipping into tubs of ice cream, ignoring the bread and butter of life, feasting on cake.

The others brought him daily bulletins.

'You won't have to miss swimming any more,' Tanya told him. 'He's giving up on Woodwork. He says he's learned enough to make bookshelves and since bookshelves is what we need, book-shelves it is.'

'Super,' said Ivan. 'A great relief.'

Nicholas said:

'You know we kept on running out of coffee and Granny's peppermints and stuff? Well, they're going to arrange for deliveries to the door every week – huge boxes filled with lovely stuff that we can eat. And Mum's gone out and bought a little green order book to keep in the kitchen. If you see something's running low, you just write it down in the order book and, lo and behold, on Tuesday it will be there in the box, just like clockwork.'

'Brilliant,' said Ivan. 'We should have thought of it years ago.'

'They've sold that antique dresser,' Sophie told him. 'The one that belonged to Granny's great-grandmother. They're going to spend the money on a much, much bigger freezer. They're going to stuff it with heavenly convenience foods.'

'Terrific!' Ivan said.

'You remember in dancing class he had such a bad time with his turns,' Nicholas confided. 'Well, he's decided to call it a day and stick to disco dancing, where turns don't matter.'

'Unless you're turning green.'

'That means that as soon as she's moved up to Intermediate Italian, which is on Tuesdays instead of Mondays, there'll be one or the other of them in most evenings, not counting dancing every Saturday.'

'Everyone needs one good night out on the town every week,' Ivan said.

Tanya rushed upstairs, bursting with the news.

'He's hiring a nurse, a private nurse, for four whole days! She's going cheap because she only qualified last week and she's so nervous. She's the daughter of somebody Natasha knows. We're going to take the car and drive up to the Lake District for a weekend and stay in real hotels!'

'*Fantastic!*'

Sophie showed him the small neat window of a hole cut in the Situations Vacant column of the newspaper.

'Here. See? She's cut it out. It's a job vacancy. It must be. The other side is just some advertisement for thermal underwear, and both of them have already got some.'

'What about Gran?'

Sophie's eyes travelled up and down the rest of the jobs advertised in the column. She said:

'You realize that with salaries like these, she could afford to pay someone else to sit with Granny and still have enough left to make working worthwhile.'

'Then good luck to her, that's what I say,' Ivan said.

Last things

Ivan sat up in bed, filling up the very last spaces in his bright red notebook. Right at the end of the *Household* section, by writing very small indeed, he managed to fit in one last short item:

Beer was sometimes used as furniture polish and might be rubbed on with a real rabbit's paw.

On the page between the chapters on *Schooling* and *Farming*, which he'd intended to leave blank, he now added:

In winter, Granny's mother and father used to be sent to school with baked potatoes which kept their hands warm on the walk, and then were eaten.

And, under that:

Children were often kept off school to work at jobs like pig-watching, bird-scaring, pea-pulling, potato-setting, fruit-picking or stone-clearing. The summer holiday is longest because, back then, the children were needed to help on the farms.

By making his letters very tall and thin, Ivan managed to slot in, halfway through *Farming*:

Farmers warned that barley in particular should never be sown before the earth was warm on your bum.

He wondered about the word 'bum', but left it in all the same. It was, after all, the word she had used when she told him.

To the chapter called *Memories*, he added:

Old Mrs H. remembered her mother saying there never used to be paint all over the roads. In fact, she could remember how odd all the new paint lines looked, till she got used to them.

And then, underneath her description of a typical birthday:

Old Mrs H. says she cannot remember being kissed or hugged by her own father, ever.

He recalled what she had told him, late one evening, about the time when Jack the Ripper was believed to be lurking round about her mother's village. He searched through for a space to write it in, but there was none left. He looked right through the notebook. It was full up. There was no room left anywhere. So, in the end, regretfully, he left it out; and after one last look through all his work, he laid the notebook down upon the chest of drawers beside his bed, for Sophie to take in to Miss Ballantyne in school, the next morning.

'Wake up, now.'

Relapse

The first time that Ivan came down the staircase, he wrapped his dressing gown more tightly around him and kept his hand on the banisters since the unusual shakiness of his legs and dizziness in his head unnerved him. He wandered through the hall into the kitchen. The only person about was his father. He saw him through the window, down at the bottom of the garden, forcing the week's last bag of rubbish into the wheelie bin. The others were all out somewhere.

Ivan trailed back along the hall and pushed open the door to his grandmother's room. At first, seeing her empty chair, he thought she wasn't there; but she was in the bed still, on her back, tiny against huge billowing pillows, like some small wrinkled white-haired manikin. She was having a very bad dream, he was quite sure of that. Her eyes were closed, her lips were dark, her face had a strange dusky flush and she was breathing fast and nervously. Her bent old fingers clawed and plucked at the sheet.

'Hello,' he said. And when she didn't wake, he said more loudly: 'Hello there, Gran. It's me again. Ivan. Back from the dead.'

Her eyelids flickered up, showing pale bluish unseeing slivers.

'Come on, Gran,' Ivan said, a little nervously. 'Wake up, now.'

He slid his arms around her and pulled. Her frail frame shook, and wisps of her hair slid out from under the small brown plastic combs with which her head was studded, and trembled as if a breeze had suddenly whirled through the room from nowhere.

'Come on, Gran. Up we go.'

He lifted her. For all that he was feeling pretty weak himself, she seemed much lighter than he remembered as he pulled her up and settled her against the pillows. She seemed to have lost the knack of anchoring herself firmly. Twice she slid back down into the bedclothes and he had to help her up all over again.

'Come *on*, Gran. Buck up, will you? What is the matter?'

She muttered something he couldn't catch.

'Gran?'

Looking down at her, he suddenly remembered something. As quickly as he could, he dragged the television across the room, tangling the lead around the legs of her armchair in his haste, and nearly toppling it from its wheeled frame.

'Look, Gran. We're missing *Solomon Street*. You'll have to catch me up on everything. I'm days behind.'

He pressed the wrong channel button on the remote control and then, trying to correct it, lost the sound by mistake. At last he got it right and turned round to draw her in with him, to watch it. To his dismay, she had slid down again and lay, eyes hovering shut, swamped in the bedclothes she was plucking at.

'Gran!'

Ivan turned the sound up higher, determined to wake her. 'Look,' he said over the noise of it, panicking. 'Angela's thinking she might be pregnant already. She's sure of it. She's checking her diary. Look, she's running to tell Marcus the news, but he's in such a foul mood about whatever it was that Daphne just said to him that he's frozen poor old Angela off. She's running off crying. She hasn't even got to tell him about the baby. Look, Gran! Tom Handley's leaving a note in that haystack for Angela to find. Now the wind's lifted and blown it out across the field into the lane. Now Daphne's found it. Typical. She'll make more trouble. Marcus is still waiting up for Angela. He's sorry about the tiff, you can tell. He didn't mean to be so horrible. Oh, no! He's noticed the time. He's looking at the clock. It's well after midnight. He's furious. He's not a bit sorry any longer. She's really going to catch it when she gets back. Oh, Gran! *Wake up!*'

He kept on at her, his voice raised over the strident blare of the television, desperate to pierce her restless, dream-ridden sleep, until his father, passing by in the hall and hearing the unmistakable undercurrent of hysteria in the pitch of his son's voice, pushed open the door and, after one quick anxious look at the old lady, took his son firmly by the arm and led him up again to his own bed.

She's not dead yet

'...quite common syndrome...' they heard the doctor's voice drone on and on as Henry led him away down the hall. '...has even been nicknamed The Old Man's Friend...severe inflammation of the mucous membrane...affects the bronchial tubes...and maxillary sinuses...the respiratory passages...resultant bronco-pneumonia.'

'There!' Tanya crowed. '*Pneumonia!* I *said* so!' She added with some relish: 'Since it was Ivan's cold she caught to start with, if Granny dies it would be fair to say that Ivan killed her.'

'Fair, yes; kind, no,' Natasha said. The notion – neither a new nor a convincing one – that Mrs Harris might die appeared to be leaving her unmoved. Sophie said, not for the first time that evening:

'You ought to tell Ivan.'

'She is not dead yet.'

'You ought to tell him before she dies.'

'She may not die.'

'You heard what he just said. He said pneumonia was called The Old Man's Friend!'

'He is not God. He isn't certain about everything.'

'He sounded pretty certain about this!'

'Tsssk! Sophie, my darling . . .'

Sophie let it drop. Her mother had, she knew, sat up for three nights in a row at the bedside. There were dark shadows round her eyes. She slouched, slovenly in her dressing gown, against the airing-cupboard door.

'Come and sit down. You look worn out.'

'I will go up and take a bath now.'

'I'll see that everything's all right down here.'

Natasha said: 'You're a good soul,' to her, and ran her fingers lightly over Sophie's hair on her way out.

Nicholas scooped Lucy up from where she was crouched eating over her bowl. He held her down firmly on his knees and stroked her fur. She kept her body tensed, ready to jump back down at the first opportunity, her eyes upon the half-full feeding dish.

'She won't purr for me. Maybe she knows.'

'She's going to hate it,' Tanya said. 'The house will be horrid and empty all day. There'll be no nice warm lap for her to sleep in. She'll miss Gran horribly, but she won't understand what's happened at all.'

'She'll understand,' said Nicholas. 'I'm sure

pets understand when their owners have died.'

'She's not dead yet,' snapped Sophie.

'Do you remember,' Tanya said suddenly, 'how, if you put your elbows on the table, she'd shake her knife at you and tell you all meat joints on the table would be carved, cooked or not?'

'She said punks looked like half-scraped carrots!'

'She used to say: "Little girl, box of paints, sucked her brush, joined the Saints!"'

'She said pyjamas should be loose in case you swelled up in the night!'

Henry came in from seeing out the doctor to find his children reeling about the kitchen, in gales of laughter, screaming:

'And do you remember when she bopped the new milkman on the head with that bottle?'

'And when she called the detective inspector a young whipper-snapper!'

'And the day she actually sat in Nicholas's paddling pool in the garden wearing that funny orange bathing suit with little frilly skirts?'

'And when Tanya showed her her brand new shoes and Granny called them "pretty little shoe-poddies" and Tanya bit her and never ever wore them again!'

'She said Mrs Herbert on *Solomon Street* was

so bandy-legged that she couldn't have stopped a pig in an entry!'

'She said when Nicholas was born he looked no bigger than half a pound of soap after a good day's wash!'

'She was so *funny!*' Nicholas said.

Tanya and Sophie stopped laughing. Their faces fell. They looked at Nicholas, still chortling away merrily, with some embarrassment. Confused, Nicholas broke off himself and asked:

'What's the matter?'

And it was Henry who had to remind him:

'She's not dead yet.'

Go and tell

Natasha told Sophie: 'Go and tell your brother his grandmother is going to die.'

'You tell him,' Sophie said, horrified.

'*You* tell him,' said Natasha. 'You'll do it right.'

Sophie went up to Ivan's room. Expressionless, like some enormous plastic doll standing there beside the bed, she informed him:

'She's going to die. It's practically certain.'

'Who says?'

'They all do.'

'Why? Can't they just give her penicillin or something?'

'I don't think it's that simple when you're so old.'

'They've *tried*, though, haven't they?'

'Oh, yes. They've tried. But it's not working.'

'She only caught a *cold*! That's all it was!'

'That's all it *was*. Then it became bronchitis. Now it's pneumonia.'

'There must be something else they can do!'

'There probably is. But she'd have to be moved into hospital, and even then it probably wouldn't work.'

'Oh.'

'And there'd be tubes and needles and rubber sheets and strange people around her and flashing machines.'

'I suppose there would.'

'I think they think she's old enough to—'

'What? Old enough to *what*, Sophie?'

'To call it a day. She's nearly eighty-eight, after all.'

'That's not that old.'

'It is that old.'

'Just from a *cold*! A stupid, stupid *cold*! If I
hadn't gone in there with my cold, if I hadn't just
wanted to finish the Granny Project, if I'd
just stayed away, she'd never have caught it!'

'You could look on the bright side. There are
loads worse ways to go. She got one of the best
because of you.'

'One of the best?'

'Pneumonia is called The Old Man's Friend.'

'Who says?'

'Everyone says. It is a well-known fact.'

'Is it?'

'Yes.'

'Is it really?'

'Yes. Yes, it is.'

He looked a little comforted. Then the raw
guilt squirmed up again in him.

'If it's so very well-known, why don't I know
it?'

Sophie said loftily:

'Your pitiful ignorance has nothing whatever to
do with the facts.'

She watched his guilt about giving his grandmother the cold wriggle and die, once and for all.
She'd broken it. He settled back, more easily,
against the pillows.

'Does it hurt?' he asked her. 'Is she in any pain?'

'I don't think so. She isn't even conscious any more.'

'She doesn't even know she's dying, then?'

'No.'

'Old Man's Friend?'

'Yes.'

'There's no point in my coming down to see her, then?'

'Not really, no.'

'I'll come down, anyway, though. I want to.'

'Right ho. I'll go and tell them you'll be down in a bit.'

'Thanks, Sophie. Good old Sophie. Thanks.'

'That's all right, comrade.'

She turned and left the room. Outside on the landing Natasha stood, eavesdropping, gnawing her fingernails, thin and tired.

She clutched her daughter as she passed and hugged her tightly.

'See?' she hissed in her ear. 'I'm never wrong. You were the one to do it. You did it right.'

Early morning

The death came some time in the middle of the night. Natasha thought of waking Henry and then decided against it. He was as tired as she was. There would be much to do the next day.

She sat alone beside the body until the early morning. Then she went quietly around the house, from bedroom to bedroom, switching the alarms on all the clocks to off, regarding each colourful, living, breathing mound of duvet with the same wonder she'd felt when each of her children was born.

Tanya, startled into wakefulness by the creak of a floorboard beside her bed, rolled over and, seeing her mother standing there, set-faced, asked nervously:

'What are you thinking?'

Natasha said:

'Life is a sigh between two secrets.'

'Blimey,' said Tanya, relieved it wasn't trouble. Pulling the duvet more tightly around her bare shoulders, she promptly went back to sleep.

At eight, Natasha rang the doctor. Then, sitting waiting beside the telephone, she looked up Funeral

Directors in the yellow pages of the phone book. A short way down the second column of firms' advertisements one stood out, boldly circled by Henry's blood-red school marking pen.

Natasha thought about the deaths of her own parents – far off deaths she had no way of picturing and had not known about until too late. She traced her finger round Henry's careful, steady, dutiful ink ring, and then tapped in the number.

Grave-faced

During the graveside funeral service, Henry listened to the words. They were quite beautiful, he thought.

He cometh up, and is cut down, like a flower; he fleeth as it were a shadow, and never continueth in one stay. Words of quiet acceptance, thought Henry. *Earth to earth, ashes to ashes, dust to dust.* And so revealing: *We give thee hearty thanks, for that it hath pleased thee to deliver this our sister out of the miseries of this sinful world.*

He wondered what the words in the French

funeral were. And the German. He thought he would ask Madame Rollet and Herr Blüchner when he ran into them in the staff room next day. There wasn't any point in asking Natasha about the Russian. She wouldn't have the faintest idea. He'd have to look that up for himself.

Nicholas was timing the funeral. It took twenty minutes. He supposed the vicar was speeding it all up a little because it was raining and Natasha, not very sensibly dressed, was looking blue with cold within a couple of minutes. Nicholas worked out, during the funeral, the cubic capacity of the hole the gravediggers had prepared. He then worked out, at various estimates of spadefuls per square metre, how many spadefuls of earth the job had involved. After, with surreptitious glances about him, he tried to estimate the number of graves in the churchyard. He squinted at the nearest row to try and work out what proportion of them were communal graves, for husbands and wives, or whole families, and should therefore be treated as more than one in his calculation. He craned about until he saw his father glaring at him. From then on he craned, but more furtively, so as not to appear inattentive. He was about to embark on the rather daunting calculation of roughly how many spadefuls of earth had been shifted in the entire history of the graveyard when, mercifully, the vicar stopped.

Tanya had never seen a coffin before, except in hearses driving by in the street. She'd heard her father saying he'd ordered the cheapest, and she had rather been expecting to see a thin plywood box with rough edges. This coffin, though, was made of creamy, grainy wood. It had shining brass handles and a brass plate. So halfway through, unable to wait till after, she whispered to Henry:

'It doesn't *look* cheap.'

'It *wasn't* cheap.'

'I thought you said it was the cheapest.'

'It was the cheapest. I didn't say that it was *cheap*.'

'It looks *expensive*.'

'It was expensive.'

'That's not very fair. You have to have a coffin. What if you're poor?'

'Tanya, it's Bonnington Cemetery we're standing in, not Speaker's Corner.'

'But Dad—'

'Sssh, Tanya. Ssshhh!'

Natasha looked across the hole in the ground

at Henry, who was in his best suit, the one he only wore for weddings and funerals and job interviews. She hadn't seen him wearing it for years. After the wind shifted slightly towards the east, the smell of mothballs from him no longer carried over to where she was standing. The rain happened to have plastered his hair down, hiding his small bald patch. He looked altogether dashing, very much like when she first met him all those years ago, at the Amnesty rally. Natasha decided she really ought to take the time, now she was free at last, to sign on at the Job Centre and join Greenpeace and apply for a place at the Open University and buy some fresh underwear. She thought she might take Sophie with her, into the city. She'd buy her a nice lunch. They'd never before had the chance to go shopping together.

Sophie could see that Ivan, still run down, was close to tears. She turned her head towards him and whispered:

'You look grave-faced.'

She winked at him, and he winked back.

Pale ivory

Natasha said, looking round the room for the twentieth time:

'Ivory. Pale ivory. I will not be argued with any longer. I am insisting.'

'Red,' Tanya pleaded. '*Please.*'

Ivan and Sophie shuffled paint colour sample cards across the floor in a ridiculous rule-free game.

'Snap!' Sophie said.

'Which?'

'Autumn Hues.'

'Well, Snap! for Beachy Golds then.'

'All right.'

'Tsssk! Hush! I am thinking.'

'Red for the *shelves*, at least.'

'Tsssk! Go away.'

'It's our room, too, now.'

Natasha flung herself into the old armchair.

'Phone the Salvation Army,' she said. 'Ask them to come and take all this stuff away.'

'You can't just give that bed away! That bed's far better than mine. Mine's nothing but lumps.'

'That chest of drawers would fit behind my door. I need more space.'

'Don't give that mirror away. Nicholas hasn't got one.'

'I want it out. All out. Every last thing. Down to the pictures on the walls and all the woollens in the drawers.'

'You're not to throw my posters out! I want them back!'

'Take them.'

'And Granny promised me that I could have all of her china ornaments!'

'Take them. The rest all goes. Today.'

'Today?'

'Now. Up you get. Sophie, put all those silly cards away at once. Carry this stuff out to the garage, every last bit. When I come back, I want the room clear and the carpets rolled.'

'Where are you going?'

'Out. Out to buy paint.'

'Red. Red, *please*. Red!'

'Pale ivory. It is decided.'

Enjoying the break

M iss Ballantyne, catching Ivan in the privacy of a school corridor, handed him back the bright red notebook containing the Granny Project.

'It was an excellent piece of work. Excellent. And, I might add, an enormous amount of work for just half a term.'

'Oh, well,' said Ivan. 'You know.'

'It's made up, quite a bit, for that fiasco earlier on. But I expect that's what you were hoping.'

'Not really,' Ivan said. 'I just sort of got carried away.'

'Well, I found it all most interesting.'

'So did I. It interested me a lot.'

'Yes.'

Ivan stood waiting for Miss Ballantyne to work her way round to it, but in the end she came straight out with:

'I understand your grandmother died last week.'

'Yes.'

'I'm very sorry.'

'That's all right. She was pretty old. She was eighty-seven, nearly eighty-eight. That's old enough to call it a day.'

'I suppose so . . .'

'And it wasn't too bad. She was quite lucky. She got pneumonia. You know – it's called "The Old Man's Friend".'

'I didn't know.'

'Didn't you?' He sounded quite surprised. 'It's a well-known fact.'

'Is it?'

'Yes. Yes, it is.'

'Well, none the less, reading your Granny Project, it became clear to me that you and she must have been very close. I expect it hurts. I expect that you miss her.'

'Not really,' Ivan said. 'In fact, I'm rather enjoying the break from her, myself.'

'Oh.'

Ivan shifted on his sneakers, and looked up at the wall clock anxiously. The second bell had already rung, and he was late.

Miss Ballantyne said:

'Well. Off you go, then.'

'Thank you.'

'And – well done, anyway. You'll see *how* well

done when you get your report, and I think you'll be pleased.'

'Thank you.'

'Well, off you go, then.'

'Right, then.'

And off he went, leaving her staring after him.

Ice-cream sundae

'I'll tell you something,' Sophie said to Tanya. 'When all these china ornaments were on Granny's dresser, I thought that they looked horrible. Really horrible. Sort of cheap and nasty. I couldn't think why you would want them. I thought you must be mad. But now, looking at them here in your room, spread out like this, all sparkly clean, I think they're absolutely beautiful. I wish I'd got some myself. They're really lovely.'

'Take one,' said Tanya.

'I didn't mean that,' Sophie said.

'I know you didn't. But go on anyway. Take one. Choose one you want. I'd like you to.'

'No. It's a collection. You keep them all.'

'Please take one,' Tanya said. 'I'd actually prefer it if I didn't have every single one of them. I'd feel much better about keeping the rest.'

'Well, if you mean it . . .'

Sophie prowled round the room, looking. She stopped in front of a tiny china ice-cream sundae, with a blob of cherry on the top, and a silver spoon.

'Can I have this one? It isn't one of your favourites, is it?'

'I like it, yes. But it isn't one of my very favourites. You have it.'

'You're sure?'

'Yes.'

'Good. I'd like to have this one.'

She picked it up and Tanya said:

'I never thought you'd pick that one.'

'Why not?'

'It isn't very—' Lost for the word, she simply shrugged.

'Grannyish?'

'Yes. That.'

'I suppose it isn't.'

'I don't suppose she ever had an ice-cream sundae in her whole childhood.'

'Maybe she did. Maybe she had one, once, and thought that it was so fantastic she bought this china ornament, just to remember.'

'Should have asked.'

'Yes.'

'Pity we didn't.'

'Right.'

'It's too late, now.'

'Never mind. Not really that important, anyway.'

'No. Still . . .'

Sherlock Holmes on TV

Nicholas swivelled the slim silver television aerial round and round. The picture failed to improve. The blurred announcer said to him:

'And now, the latest in our series of Sherlock Holmes films.'

Desperate, Nicholas switched him off, ran down the hall and pushed open the door, shouting:

'Gran! Gran, are you watching Sherlock Holmes?'

The paint smell hit him. And the sheer lightness. The windows without their curtains, seemed enormous; the floor, without the carpet, looked acres wide. It was a strange room.

He turned back to the hall and bumped into Henry. He shouted at him:

'Where is the other bloody television?'

Henry stared at him. He'd never heard this son swear before.

'*What* did you just say?'

Nicholas stamped his foot and yelled at him:

'Where have you bloody well put it?'

'Put what?'

'The other television. The television that used to be in here. The spare one.'

'Granny's?'

'Yes.'

'It's gone back to the shop. It was only rented.'

Nicholas burst into tears.

'What is the matter?' Henry said. He put his hand on Nicholas's shoulder and fiercely Nicholas shook it straight off.

Henry looked past his son into the light airy, empty room. He smelled the fresh paint smell.

'You forgot.'

'I *didn't* forget!' Nicholas screamed at him. 'I did *not forget*! I just want to watch *Sherlock Holmes*! I'm *missing* it! I'm missing the *start*!'

He ran back to the other room. He sat hunched on the floor, close to the screen, where he was forbidden to sit. He had to concentrate doubly hard on the blurred, drifting picture before him till Henry, following him in, managed to tune it a little better.

Comrade

Sophie and Ivan stood side by side on the grass a few steps from the grave. Far away, on the other side of the churchyard, Tanya and Nicholas were leapfrogging over the tombstones, shrieking brave challenges to one another. Natasha had gone off after Henry, around the church building, to put the bucket back under the tap.

Sophie said:

'Ivan, if Granny hadn't died, and we could start again, would you still vote for keeping her at home?'

'Yes,' Ivan said.

'Just the same?'

'No, not just the same. Not with the system

where they did all the work, and hated it. Or with the one where I did. I'd opt for the final negotiated settlement, that plan you all had just worked out together before she got sick.'

'That compromise?'

'That's right. That's what I would have voted for.'

'I would have voted for that, too. I think we all would. That was all right, that plan. It would have worked. We should have thought of that before.' She kicked the grass morosely, and added: 'If we had thought of that before, I never would have ended up telling those lies. We were stupid, we were.'

'Right. We were stupid.'

'Stupid.'

'One consolation, though. We're never going to be that stupid again.'

'Oh, no?'

'No. Because I'm going to make it my business.'

'Your business?'

'I'm going to be a professional negotiator. I've decided, I think. It's a way of trying to make things better that isn't too sad and it isn't too slow. I've been thinking about it a lot recently. I'll work my way up through the unions—'

'Like Grandfather.'

'Yes, like him. But then I'm going to branch out. Hostage negotiations. Arguments over boundaries. Things to get settled before wars can come to an end. Because negotiation's the way forward now, you know, Sophie, not simple confrontation. So I'm going to sort things out for a living. Things like whether Granny should have gone in that Home or not, but even messier.'

'You'd probably be good at it.'

'I think I would.'

'You would.'

Sophie looked over at Tanya and Nicholas, still scissor-kicking over one gravestone after another.

'Ivan, do you believe there's any purpose in life?'

'Not really, no.'

'But you've decided what you're going to do.'

'It's not a purpose. I just thought I might try to improve things a bit.'

'That is a purpose.'

'I suppose it is.'

'You've got one, then.'

'I suppose I have.'

'A sort of Project for Life.'

'Don't let Natasha hear. She'll blow me up.'

They laughed.

Sophie went back to looking at the grave, set under the lowest branches of an enormous yew tree. There was no headstone yet, because the hump of earth still had to settle; but there were bunches of cut flowers tossed about it, to hide the sheer rawness of the fresh dug soil.

'I don't know why they bothered to plant things. They won't get any flowers to grow on there. It's far too shady. It won't get any sun at all, ever, under that yew.'

Sophie's eyes lifted from the grave to the dark sprawling fronds of the huge tree above it. She looked up, layer by spreading layer, to the very top.

'Ivan!'

She was appalled.

'Ivan! You see what's going to happen, don't you? They've buried her down there, six feet under. That's a rule, so they *must* have! They've buried her right down among the tree roots! You realize what's going to happen to Granny? She's going to get sucked right up that tree!'

Ivan felt sick. He looked down, gaining time, checking that she was right about it, then up again. The tree towered over them both, huge, ancient and magnificent. It dwarfed the two of them, alive, and made a mockery of the idea of one old lady's tiny body resisting it.

Ivan took a deep breath and battened down nausea.

'She'd like that,' he said as calmly as he could.

'*Like* it!'

'Sure.'

He comforted his sister about the grave just as she comforted him about the pneumonia. 'I'm sure she'd like that. Why shouldn't she? She once told me she liked to feel a part of things. I think that she'd be very pleased to think she would become part of a tree.'

'Do you?'

'Yes. Yes, I do.'

'*Really*?'

'Yes.'

He could see she was still dubious, so he added:

'Certainly. No question about it.'

And she was comforted.

'That's all right, then.'

They stood side by side and watched as Henry and Natasha came in sight again at last around the side of the church. As they came closer, Henry whistled across, and Tanya and Nicholas began to leapfrog over towards them.

Before it was too late, Ivan said hastily:

'Don't tell them all, though. Don't mention it. Please don't say anything on the ride home. I simply couldn't stand it.'

Sophie said cheerily:

'Right ho, then, comrade.'